DOGS FROM ILLUSION

CHUSMA HOUSE

CHUSMA HOUSE PUBLICATIONS

I

ISBN: 0-9624536-5-X

Library of Congress
Catalog Card Number: 94-94169

Cover Illustration, Graphic Design and Typography
by
Hiram Duran Alvarez

CHUSMA
HOUSE

CHUSMA HOUSE PUBLICATIONS

PO Box 467
San José, CA 95103
(408) 947-0958

First Printing
Printed in Atzlán

Episodes

For JJ

My Down Syndrome baby brother, who has never known
hate—only love. His courage and strength are inspirational.

EPISODE I
The Wedding Dance

The Texas drawl of President Lyndon Baines Johnson comes over the radio: "When we line them up at the reception centers to fit them for their uniforms, we don't say, what is your church? What is your political affiliation? What section of the country do you live in and who was your grandpa? We say, give him size 42."

A large, overweight farm labor contractor stands at the end of the sugar beet rows, listening to a transistor radio placed next to his ear as he waits for the three remaining workers to finish thinning their rows.

Down the rows, three figures are stooped over and working assiduously. In their hands is the nefarious short-handle hoe known as "el cortito." The hoe has a twelve inch handle and a four to five inch blade. They whack away at clumps of short, dark-green sugar beet tops with one hand and pull out the excess foliage with the other. They leave only two or three plants intact. All of the weeds that surround the sugar beets must also be cleared.

Ese, Chuco and Machete are racing to see who can finish thinning his row first. "Voy a chingar,"[1] yells Chuco. This is all the challenge Machete needs in order to make a last effort to win the contest. After reaching the end, he gleams with relief knowing that this may well be the last time he will chop sugar beets.

All three are very good at thinning sugar beets and most other farm work since they were children, but today, Machete won the race. For their efforts, they have earned fifteen dollars apiece. They will give

---

1. "I'm going to kick ass,"

half of it to their mothers and keep the rest. Machete waits several seconds for his friends to reach the end of the rows.

"Fuck, Hijola man, these rows were hard," says Chuco.

"Estan más tupidos que la chingada,"[2] concludes Ese, while he takes off the bandana tied around his head and wipes the sweat from his neck and forehead. As he combs his short black hair back, he reviews the finished rows. He compares them to the unthinned rows, how precise and orderly they are in contrast. Like most farmwork, thinning beets is low paid and considered unskilled work. Yet, not many people can endure the physical toil or are skillful enough to be productive.

"Do you guys wear a size 42?" asks the farm labor contractor.

"What the fuck you talking about…¿estas loco o qué Cheno?"[3] retorts Ese.

As the three prepare to leave for their car, the bombastic overweight connoisseur of beans, chile and tortillas asks, "So you fools are going to Viet Nam tomorrow?"

"That's right. What's it to you, asshole?" asks Machete.

"Hey muchachos, why get mad at me? It's not my fault you got to go to Viet Nam and fight for the gringos."

"We don't give a shit what you think, Cheno. We just want to get paid before we leave. And if you don't pay us, we're going to kick your ass," answers Machete.

"Ha," says Cheno with a laugh, "you punks think you can do it?"

"Don't pay us and find out," answers Machete.

"Jesus, you guys are edgy. Why are you working out here anyway? If I were you, I'd be out with the girls."

"That's none of your business, baboso.[4] By the way, why don't you just pay us right now?" asks Chuco.

---

2. "They were thicker than shit,"
3. …are you crazy or what Cheno?
4. stupid

"I don't have the money right now. Come to the house about three o'clock and I'll have it. And if you make it back from Viet Nam, I'll also have your hoes sharpened and ready for you too," mocks Cheno.

"Go to hell. Just pay us," answers Machete with indignation. Machete has inherited the physical characteristics of his Yaqui ancestors and the temperament of his Pancho Villa forefathers. Square shoulders, medium height, cinnamon brown skin and more than a hint of Asiatic facial features. Machete is one crazy and irascible vato, especially when he is drinking.

Machete had been a precocious kid. He had gotten drunk for the first time at the age of twelve. At thirteen, the finest thirty-year old widow in Illusion had taken his virginity. He would revel with boys older than he. On the first occasion he had gotten drunk, the older boys taunted him to such a point that he went into a rage. He attacked them, but they were too big and too many for him to fight. When he realized this, he ran down the block to his house, into his father's tool shed, and brought out a machete.

With machete in hand, he ran to his buddies. By the time he returned, everyone was in Bubble's car. Still in a rage, he ran to attack the car. Bubbles would let Machete get close to the car, then accelerate just enough so Machete could not reach the car. Then he would slow down and allow Machete to think he was catching up.

All the time the boys were taunting him with insults such as: "Your tío Filo is a maricon. Your grandma wears tirantes with Beatle boots. Tu abuelo no se baña y tiene piojos. Your Tía Chata has big chichis and your sister Tencha gives nalga to everybody...your cousin Crow just died."[5]

This went on for six blocks. With all the commotion, several of the neighborhood dogs had joined in on the chase. Realizing that he

5. Your uncle Filo is a faggot. Your grandma wears suspenders with Beatle boots. Your grandfather doesn't take a bath and has lice. Your aunt Chata has big tits and your sister Tencha gives ass to everybody.

wasn't going to catch up to the car, his face flushed with anger and hate, Machete attacked the dogs that were barking alongside of him. He lashed at them with his machete. All the dogs scattered, except for Terror—the meanest and largest German Shepherd in the neighborhood—who lunged at Machete.

Terror knocked Machete down and tried to bite him, but Machete's leather jacket kept the dog's bites from penetrating. He was able to fend the dog off. After struggling with the dog for several minutes, Machete finally managed to take a good swing at Terror and bust one of his eyes out. Stricken with shock and pain, Terror ran off yelping. Hence, the name Machete.

That same year, Chuco and Machete were expelled from Junior High School because they lost the litigation with the principal over the rights to his parking place. They parked an abandoned, stolen car that they had found while hunting rabbits in the country in the principal's parking space.

Chuco is quieter than Machete and Ese, but capricious and quixotic. His physical characteristics are a mixture of his Indian and Spanish forefathers. His nose is straight and his eyes are like a coyote's. His hair is dark brown; he is lighter skinned and taller than Ese or Machete. Everyone calls him Chuco because of his fastidious, neo-pachuco dress: Starched khaki pants, French-Toe Stacey Adams shoes, white J.C. Penny T-shirt and an immaculately pressed shirt worn untucked.

Chuco was an outstanding wrestler at the 165 pound weight. However, he had been suspended from high school several times because of his propensity for wearing his shirt tail out, as well as for speaking Spanish on campus. By his senior year in high school, his morale was demoralized by the lack of recognition for his wrestling accomplishments from the school. Therefore, he didn't bother to go out for wrestling. He and Machete were finally expelled from school for not attending class.

They didn't attend class because they were bored, but they also had to help support their families by irrigating the cotton fields at night. By lunch time, they would show up with Decay Germs, who was called this because he had a severe case of pyorrhea. They'd loiter in the halls and create general havoc. Things were better for them now because they didn't have to make a pretense of attending school. However, they would still go to school at lunch time and after classes to flirt with the girls.

Ese, in contrast to Chuco and Machete, was much more of a school conformist. He didn't miss much school and was an above average middle distance runner on the track team. He had been a Boy Scout and was considered to be a "coconut," white in the inside and brown on the outside. He attended catechism until his junior year in high school and is a devout catholic.

Shorter and darker than either Chuco or Machete, Ese has coarse, jet-black hair with large eyes. He is jovial and has a happy-go-lucky personality. But at times, when he is frustrated or upset, he may become petulant and mean. He is called Ese after his father. His father was at one time a hard-core Pachuco and would use the word "ese" more than frequently in his speech. So Ese is actually Ese Jr.

All three soldiers' families had arrived in Illusion in the early 1920's, when Mexican labor was needed to work in the fields of Central California. Many new towns were populated and incorporated in this area because of the 1902 Federal Reclamation Act, which provided for water projects and led to an increase in agriculture production.

Machete's family had come from Chihuahua to escape political persecution because of his father and uncle's fighting under Pancho Villa. Chuco's family had migrated from Los Angeles. Ese's family is originally from Texas, where they had lived since it was Mexico. Chuco and Ese's fathers and uncles had fought in World War II and Korea; so for them, it is a family tradition to fight in U.S. wars.

Chuco and Machete have been drafted; and of the two, Machete is more reluctant than Chuco to serve in the army. Machete doesn't think it is his war and doesn't want to leave his fiancée, Tweedy. Chuco wouldn't have volunteered for the service, but doesn't fight the draft either. Ese, on the other hand, has volunteered for the army because he feels it is his patriotic duty to fight in Viet Nam. Chuco is unattached and unconcerned about serious romantic relationships. Ese's girlfriend, Muñeca, has dropped him, and he now goes out with Chanclas who loves Ese, but he doesn't love her because he is still in love with Muñeca.

They all get in Machete's two-tone, cherry red and white 55 Chevy and Ese says, "As the sheepherder would say, 'let's get the flock out of here.'"

They drive toward the river store to buy beer. Ese has a military I.D. that indicates he is twenty-one, instead of nineteen. He knew he was going to have a problem buying beer when he was home on leave, so he came up with the idea of reporting his I.D. missing and falsifying his birthdate.

After buying the beer, they head for their favorite drinking spot they call "cabletree," where the sheriff seldom bothers them and they can drink beer in peace.

Along the way, the radio is blasting away. They pass green fields of sugar beets and newly planted cotton. The cotton is being irrigated, so the wet dirt gives off a lush, damp smell which makes them feel cooler.

Chuco lights up a marijuana joint and takes a deep, healthy drag, then passes it to Ese sitting in the back seat. Ese takes the cigarette he is smoking and places it on his left ear, in order to take the joint. After they finish the joint, Chuco asks, "What's that funny smell? It smells like burning wool or something."

"Yeah, it smells fucked up," says Machete. "Maybe it's your Pendleton burning."

Ese looks around and says, "No, it ain't the shirt." As he finishes the sentence, he grabs his ear and starts slapping the side of his head to turn off the cigarette and yells, "Hijo de su pinche madre[6] it's my hair! Como soy pendejo, baboso y buey."[7] They all laugh hysterically. Machete is so overtaken by laughter that he must stop the car. After laughing like idiots for several minutes, Chuco says, "Man, that's some good laughing weed."

"You ain't lying," agrees Chuco with tears in his eyes.

They reach cabletree and park under the immense shade given by the giant oak tree.

"I think I'm going to miss this place," says Ese.

"Well, you'd better forget about this place for a while because it ain't going to do you any good once we're in Viet Nam," advises Chuco.

"I don't think I want to go over there…I've been thinking about not going over at all. My mother tells me that some of our relatives in Mexico will take care of me over there."

"That's bullshit, Machete," says Ese while he picks up a rock and throws it at the water, "What the fuck you going to do in Mexico? It's real poor over there. Why do you think people come over here to work?"

"Yeah, I know, but why should I go fight some putos[8] I don't even

6. "Son of a bitch,
7. I sure am a stupid jackass.
8. assholes

7

know?"

"Well, it's too late to think about that now… we've got a job to do," says Ese.

"Right," agrees Chuco. "Forget all that noise. Let's party and get fucked up. You know you've got more huevos[9] than that."

After recounting the many good times they had at cabletree, they ride back to town. Chuco is the first one dropped off.

"I'll pick you up at eight o'clock for the wedding dance," Chuco tells Ese as he gets out of the car.

"Don't you think that Chuco's house looks like the one that the Beverly Hillbillies used to live in back in the hills?" Ese says to Machete as they drive off.

"It does, huh!" replies Machete as they both laugh.

Ese gets out of the car when they arrive at the front of his house. "See you at the dance, carnal,"[10] says Ese. He walks to the front door of his house and almost trips on a dirty sheepdog that looks like a dirty rug laying across the doorway. "Pinche perro baboso,[11] move dummy," says Ese grinning.

As he walks inside, his five-year-old sister, Ranita, is watching Bullwinkle cartoons. She is a petite girl with dark round eyes which are perfectly embedded on her cherubic face. "Hey, baby sister, look what I've got for you," he tells her as he gently throws her a Snickers candy bar.

Ranita catches the candy bar and says, "Look brother, it's your favorite cartoon guy, Tudor Toytle."

Ese looks towards the television and sees Tudor Turtle caught in a crossfire of bullets frantically yelling, "Help Mr. Wizard, help Mr. Wizard, I need to get out of here." With the shake of a wand, the old

---

9. balls
10. brother,"
11. Stupid fucking dog,

wizard brings the scared turtle home.

"Turn the TV to the news, baby sister," asks Ese. Ranita does as she is told.

Walter Cronkite appears on the TV. He narrates, while footage of US soldiers zigzagging across a rice paddy under a fusillade of bullets, is shown on the screen, "These are soldiers of the 1st Infantry Division in a fierce fire fight with elements of the 405 Viet Cong Regiment."

"Is that what you are going to be doing brother?" asks the sister.

"Don't believe that stuff mija,[12] they're only playing. It's just for fun," consoles Ese.

"Then maybe we'll get to see you on TV too?"

"Yeah, maybe you will. And if I do come out, I'll be sure to wave to you. I'm going to take a shower and then go to sleep. Tell mom to wake me up when it's time to eat."

Ese goes to bed and has the same horrifying dream he's had since Muñeca broke off their relationship. The dream begins with he and Muñeca standing before an altar, with a priest marrying them. Ese is astonished to watch the priest slowly transform into a corpse as he performs the ceremony. Ese then turns to Muñeca and she is also dead. He knows they are dead because everything is a bloody purple. He turns around, and everyone in the pews points to him and say in unison, "Look he's dead, he's dead, esta muerto," and they begin to laugh at him. Ese is petrified and embarrassed because he's dead and everyone can see his virgin soul.

"Despierta hijo,"[13] says his mother as she wakes him. "Parece que tuvites una pesadilla."[14]

Ese is covered with sweat and tells her, "It's O.K. amá. ¿Ya está

12. little one
13. "Wake up son, "
14, It looks like you were having a nightmare."

la cena?"[15]

"Sí, hice enchiladas."[16]

Ese dresses and has dinner with his parents and his four younger sisters and brothers. Nothing is mentioned about Ese going to Viet Nam, but an intense, yet subtle, apprehension engulfs the family.

After dinner, Ese sits in the living room waiting for Chuco to pick him up. After a while, his little sister hears the honk from Chuco's car. She looks out the window and loudly announces, "It's Chuco. He's here...está aquí," she says as she waves to Chuco from the window.

"Ya me voy amá.[17] I'll be back right after the dance."

His mom knows that this is a formality and that he will not return until the morning to pick up his duffel bag. She knows how restless and ill at ease he has been, from the time he was in her womb, and even more so since his breakup with Muñeca.

Once again he almost trips over the shaggy dog as he walks out the door. "Pinche perro pendejo,"[18] curses Ese. "Let's go to the big 'L' and get some pisto,"[19] he tells Chuco as he gets in the 53 Buick. Chuco readily complies.

They buy a six pack of beer and a pint of tequila at the liquor store, then cruise around the small town. They drive around two basic routes. One takes them down the magnolia-lined main street, around the park and high school. The other route is through the Mexican neighborhood where the streets are full of potholes. The contrast between the white and the Mexican side of town is great. The white neighborhood has nice middle-class homes with neatly trimmed lawns and sidewalks in front of them. The Mexican side has no sidewalks

---

15. Is supper ready?"
16. "Yes, I made enchiladas."
17. "I'm leaving mom
18. "Stupid fucking dog,"
19. booze,"

and some of the homes don't even have indoor plumbing.

The cultural differences between the two groups is astounding. In the summer, for example, the white people quietly stay inside their air conditioned homes. While in the Mexican side, everyone is outside sitting out in their yards. Children play games on the streets. There is constant commotion between households. Even the dogs are different. In the white side, the dogs are kept in a fenced backyard or even inside the house. In the Mexican barrio, dogs wander loosely, and no self-respecting household would allow a dog inside the house.

"Turn the radio up," asks Ese when he hears Junior Walker and the All Stars play the song "Shotgun." They ride around for an hour before they decide it's about time they go to the dance.

When they enter the Veteran's Hall the music is blaring with the usual repertoire of cumbias, rancheras, corridos, oldies and rock-and-roll. Once inside, Chuco hears someone yell to him, "Órale primo,[20] come over here." Chuco turns to where the voice is coming from, and he sees his primo Prieto waving for him.

"It's my primo," he tells Ese. "I'm going to see what he wants." It takes him a few minutes to reach Prieto, not because it is far, but because he greets several people along the way. Chuco, Ese and Machete are very well-liked in the community. Of course, they also have a few enemies. Chuco reaches Prieto and asks him, "¿Que pasa, primo?"[21]

"You'd better watch it tonight," warns Prieto with his hoarse voice. "I was drinking with some of the vatos[22] outside, when Wolfman, Pigeon and Craterface came around. Pichon started talking about how he is going to kick your ass because you've been going out with his

---

20. What's up cousin
21. What's happening cousin
22. dudes

11

ruca,[23] Sleepy Eyes. You know how those vatos are; they'll rat pack you in a heartbeat, primo."

"Que chingue su madre Pichon;[24] I'll kick his ass."

"Well I thought I'd better warn you," concludes Prieto.

On the other side of the hall, Ese is drinking a beer when he sees Machete walk in with his fiancée, Tweedy. She is a small, thin girl with pearl white teeth and elegant features. He walks over to them and asks them if they would like a drink. They say they would, so Ese goes over to the bar and brings a beer for Machete and a wine-cooler for Tweedy.

"Where's Chuco?" asks Machete.

"Over there," points Ese to the dance floor. "Anda quemando más llanta que la chingada."[25] On the dance floor, Chuco is doing the Illusion two-step to the tune of "Louie, Louie," with Sleepy Eyes. She is a sensuous girl with huge drooping eyes and a bubble butt.

The night passes quickly. Towards the end of the dance, Ese has gotten together with Chanclas and plans to leave with her. When the dance is over, the lights turn on, and people blink their eyes to adjust to the bright lights.

The three friends gather to make sure everything is taken care of for the night and for the next morning. "It looks pretty good for tonight, vatos. Chanclas tells me it's O.K. to go to her crib to spend the night because her kid is over her mom's house. And tomorrow morning my brother, The Gang, is going to take us to the airport."

"Don't look behind you, Ese, but isn't that Gypsy, Chanclas' older sister, the one you've been boning too?" asks Machete.

"Don't be bullshitting me, Machete," says Ese with sudden fear.

---

23. chick
24. "Pichon can go fuck his mama;
25. "He's dancing up a fucking storm."

"He's not loco.[26] She just walked in with curlers on her head," confirms Chuco. "And she looks pissed-off."

Gypsy spots Chanclas talking with Sleepy Eyes and Tweedy. She quickly concludes that her sister is leaving with Ese. She storms toward Ese in a menacing trot. "You fucking bastard!" she yells as she brings her blue purse up to hit Ese. He moves just in time to avoid the first swing of the purse. She is not to be taken lightly because she is a well built woman and is used to working hard in the fields. She is ferocious and becomes further enraged when Ese is able to side-step her purse attack.

"I'll kill you, you fucking bastard. What are you doing with my little sister? Wolfdaddy was right; you are screwing my little sister. And you ain't even worth a fuck for fucking with your little hamster dick ... con esa vergita de pajaro que tienes. No llegas y hasta eres joto,"[27] she says this with her eyes bulging like a pitbull's. She is so fanatically concentrated on Ese that she overlooks that she is being held back by her friends.

Machete and Chuco are enjoying every moment of the circus. But Machete tells Ese, "Get out of here before her brothers come over and start throwing chingazos[28] with us."

Ese leaves with Chanclas. "We'd better go out to cabletree because if we go to your chante,[29] your sister will probably go over there looking for us."

When they get to the car, Chanclas asks Ese, "What have you been doing with my sister? Have you been doing it with her?"

Ese lies and says, "Hell no, she's just a nut. She's been trying to go out with me for a long time; honest and hope to die if I'm lying. Let's

---

26. crazy
27. ...with that little bird dick of yours. You don't rate and your even a faggot.
28. blows
29. house

get out of here."

As soon as Ese leaves, the police arrive and question Chuco and Machete. "What happened here?" roughly asks one of the cops, called Junior, but all of the raza [30] call him Puñetas.[31] They call him Puñetas because Chuco once caught Junior masturbating the schools billy goat mascot. He also has it in for Chuco because Chuco gave him a couple of black eyes during their freshman year in high school.

No one says anything because in the Chicano community, police are generally viewed as an outside hostile force. Some of this attitude can be attributed to the historical conflict between Chicanos and gringo law. "What are you doing here, Chuco? I thought you were supposed to go to Viet Nam? I bet you're AWOL. Where is that other clown you hang around with? He's probably smoking marijuana in the parking lot. I should take you in for being AWOL, but I'd rather see you in Viet Nam; maybe you'll get killed."

"You're such a bad dude, why don't you come with us to Nam?" jeeringly rebuts Chuco.

"Now you know I couldn't do that. I've got to stay here and make sure all you Meskins don't take over, or else we won't even have to worry about the commies taking over. Everybody out of here now," barks Junior, "or I'm going to take you all in." With that warning, the hall is cleared.

"Ahí nos vemos mañana," [32] Machete tells Chuco.

They leave in opposite directions towards their cars. Halfway down the block, a car slows down alongside Chuco and Sleepy Eyes, and a voice asks, "What you doing with my jaina, puto?" [33]

It's Pichon and his buddies, realizes Chuco. "You don't own this

---

30. Chicanos
31. Jerk-Off
32. "We'll see each other tomorrow,"
33. broad, asshole?"

ruca," answers Chuco.

"Ah fuck," sighs Sleepy Eyes. "Everything's O.K. Chuco. I'll just go with him."

"Chale,[34] it ain't O.K. I'm going to kick your ass puto," says Pichon with a sneer as he gets out of the car. Pichon is somewhat smaller than Chuco, but is known to either knife people or gang up on people with his friends.

"Shit, now I know why they call you Pigeon. You've got a Pigeon head," says Chuco as he sees Pichon's head against the moonlight.

Without warning, Pichon kicks Chuco in the leg and the fight begins. Pichon is no match for Chuco. Chuco wrestles him to the ground and begins to pound on him. Suddenly, Chuco feels a kick to his head and falls to the side. Craterface and Wolfdaddy begin to pummel Chuco.

"Here comes the police!" yells Sleepy Eyes as a police car comes to an abrupt halt. The fight is so furious that it resembles a dog and cat fight in the cartoons. Sleepy Eyes' words are not heard.

Junior gets off of the car and says, "Well I'll be. Ain't this a nice scene? Chuco getting his ass kicked by his own compadres."[35]

"Stop them," pleads Sleepy Eyes.

"Not yet, little tamale. I want to see Chuco get his butt really kicked." Junior lets them fight until they've done some serious damage to Chuco.

"That's enough Mexicoons," says Junior as he kicks Chuco's opponents off. "Get the fuck out of here or I'm going to run all of you in." Chuco's opponents get in their car and scamper off.

Junior walks over to where Chuco is lying. He shines his flashlight on Chuco's face. His right eye is swollen shut. His nose is bleeding

---

34. "No,
35. buddies

profusely and one of his front teeth is missing. Chuco is in physical shock and immobile and does not yet feel the pain.

"You aren't as tough as you thought, huh, Poncho?" says Junior with a sadistic smile.

"Fuck you," says Chuco.

"Why you fucking greaser-spic-son-of-a-bitch," says Junior as he kicks Chuco in the ribs. He grabs Chuco from the collar and throws him in the car.

EPISODE II
Doña Chole's Magic

Ese and Chanclas have driven out to cabletree in order to avoid Gypsy, who will stake out Chanclas' house. After they finish copulating, they drive around Chanclas' house a couple of times to make sure Gypsy has gone home. Once inside the house, they have another round of sex. After they finish, they lay next to each other and Chanclas asks Ese, "Aren't you escared about going to Viet Nam?"

"Kind of...sort of. But I try not think about it too much because it won't do any good. Except for the other day when I did think about it, I went over to the bruja doña Chole." [1]

"She's not a bruja; she's a curandera [2] and she's my mother's comadre."

"To me she's a bruja and that's why I went to her. Anyhow, I told her I needed a good luck charm to help me out in Viet Nam. She asked me if I had a girlfriend, and I told her I did. She asked me what your name was and if we made love. So I told her your name and that we make love. Then I gave her ten dollars."

"You're so stupid. Why did you tell her my name? Now she'll tell my mother. You're so stupid."

"Come on, babe, I didn't mean it. I didn't know she knew your jefita. [3] Anyhow, she told me to do something weird. Don't get mad, but she told me to take some of your little pelitos [4] from down there," says Ese patting her vagina. "And to put them in a plastic baggy and take them with me to Viet Nam."

---

1. witch doña Chole."
2. healer
3. mother
4. hairs

"You're sick. You're stupid y estas menso."[5]

"Come on, babycakes. Do you love me? If you do, you'll let me do it. It won't hurt. All I need is to take thirteen of them."

"No! What you need are thirteen cachetadas baboso."[6]

"Come on, chulita,[7] if you really love me, you'll do it. Don't you want me to come back?"

"Pero me va a doler."[8]

"It'll only hurt for a little bit, sugarcakes. And if I die over there… it's not like I won't appreciate what you've done for me."

She gives in to Ese because she likes and pities him.

---

5. and dumb."
6. slaps idiot."
7. pretty one,
8. "But its going to hurt me."

EPISODE III
The Party

After the dance, Machete takes Tweedy home. She lives a few miles outside of town. She sits next to him in the car and continually kisses him on the side of his face as Machete drives. "I love you so much. I wish we could get married right now," says Tweedy as she looks at him with amorous eyes.

"I know, baby, but you know it's better to wait until I get back," says Machete, feeling a knot in his Adam's apple.

"I'll wait as long as it takes. I'll pray for you and write you everyday. I just hope this year goes by fast," she says, swallowing the anguish in her voice.

Machete slows the car down and makes a right turn onto a dirt road. He drives to an abandoned barn and parks behind it. This is their place for romance. They begin to caress and kiss one another. Tweedy's heart pounds erratically as Machete puts his hands under her dress. She takes his hand away and he says with disappointment, "What's wrong, baby?"

"No lo puedemos hacer esta noche," [1] she says as he buries her face on his shoulder. "Porque traigo la luna." [2]

Machete at first feels angry but calms himself and tells her, "I understand, babe." He knows that Tweedy is very traditional and will not have sex with him when she is on her menstrual cycle. He doesn't ask her to perform sexual acts, other than coitus, because he doesn't feel that it's right for his future wife to do such things. His only regret is that he didn't anticipate this, or else he would have arranged to have

---

1. "We can't do it tonight,"
2. "Because I'm on my period."

sex with another girl later that night. They continue petting for a short while before he drives her home.

When they arrive at Tweedy's house, there is a party in progress. "Oh, I forgot that it's my uncle's birthday. Let's go inside," says Tweedy inviting Machete in.

After they get off the car, they walk into the house with Machete's arms proudly around Tweedy's shoulder. A couple of dozen, mostly middle-aged, people are either in the kitchen or the living room. Beer and liquor are plentiful and everyone is having a grand time. Tweedy's father, a small, wily man with crossed eyes, approaches Machete and hands him a beer then announces loudly, "Everybody, todos por favor, can I have your attention. I'd like to introduce my future son-in-law who is going to Viet Nam in the morning." Everyone looks toward Tweedy and Machete. "Join me in wishing them a happy future together," says the father raising his glass of whiskey.

"To a good and happy marriage," say some of the people as they toast in honor of Tweedy and Machete. With that done, the music is turned on and Tweedy and Machete are congratulated by many of the people there. As one of Tweedy's uncle's gives Machete a hug, Machete notices Cheno, the labor contractor, through the screen door outside, drinking next to a tree with a couple of his buddies.

"I'll be right back," he tells Tweedy. "I've got to to talk to this guy that's outside. "It won't take long." Machete walks outside and approaches Cheno, who is quite drunk.

"Well, if it isn't our little soldadito," says Cheno jeeringly. "You ready to get your culo blown up in Viet Nam?"

"No le pongas atención, está borracho," [3] says one of Cheno's companions to Machete.

---

3. "Don't pay attention to him because he's drunk,"

"A mi me importa verga lo que pienses, pinche viejo pansón,"[4] says Machete with extreme animosity. "Paganos la feria[5] that you owe us for chopping beets," he says as he moves closer to Cheno.

"Where are the other stooges that you hang around with? Y ultimamente,[6] I don't owe you any money. Pero si quieres,[7] I'll give some feria to fuck that pretty little chiquita banana you're going to marry," says Cheno.

"O sí,"[8] says Machete his face glowering with rage. Without warning, Machete attacks Cheno with a pocket knife and cuts him across his belly.

Cheno remains standing with intense astonishment, watching his wound."Vete de aquí, Machete,"[9] Tweedy's father tells Machete as he rushes over. "I saw and heard everything. Este Cheno pendejo es muy osicón,[10] and he deserves what you did to him for talking like that about my daughter. Somebody already called the jura y van estar aquí en un poquito. Cheno no te va poner dedo porque él sabe que yo y mis carnales no lo chingamos despúes."[11]

Machete sees the police cars racing toward the house, gets in his car and makes a quick exit. As he drives he figures that it's probably better that he leave like this so he won't have to go through a painful farewell with Tweedy. He feels content with a sense of accomplishment because he did something that many people have wanted to do to Cheno for a long time.

When he arrives home, he parks behind his father's toolshed and

---

4. "I don't give a dick what you think, you old fat fucker,"
5. "Pay us the dough
6. and ultimately,
7. But if you want, I'll give you some money
8. "Oh yeah,"
9. "Get out of here Machete,"
10. This stupid Cheno has a big mouth,
11. cops are going to be here shortly. Cheno won't put the finger on you because he knows me and my brothers will kick his ass if he does."

washes his face and hands with water from a water hose. He dries himself with his shirt and walks toward the backdoor of the house. As he walks, he notices the lights of the kitchen go on. Es amá y apuesto que apá también se levanto. De cincho ya son las cinco de la mañana porque esaes la hora que se levantan. Qué pronto se fue la noche,[12] he thinks.

"Buenos dias, hijo. ¿A poco te andabas peliendo?"[13] asks his mother, noticing that he was probably in some sort of scuffle as he walks in through the kitchen door.

"No, ama. Unos muchachos se andaban peliando y yo traté de pararlos,"[14] he tells her. For the first time, he observes the wrinkles on her face and realizes she's getting old.

"Cuantas veces te he dicho que, si nos son tus propios hermanos, que no te andes metiendo en pleitos de otros,"[15] admonishes his father who is sitting at the table. "Asi igual, seria mejor que no vayas a pelear con los chinos. Esa no es bronca de nosotros. Pero ni modo. Si no vas, el gobierno te manda para la prisión."[16]

"Has lo que recomiende mi hermana Nacha…que vayas con ella para México y asi no tienes que ir para la guerra,"[17]

"Amá, como le dije antes, la pobrecita de la tía Nacha apenas esta, y de todos modos no hay trabajos alla. Toda la gente se viene a trabajar para acá. Y también, si mi voy para Méxcio, ya no puedo venir para

---

12. It's mom, I bet dad is also up. It's a cinch it's five in the morning because that's what time they get up. The night went by fast, he thinks

13. "Good morning son. Were you in a fight?

14. "No mom. Some other boys were fighting and I tried to stop them,"

15. "How many times have I told you that unless it's your own brother fighting, don't get into other people's fights.

16. "Just like it would be better for you not to go fight the Chinese. That's not our brawl. But what can we do? If you don't go, the government will send you to prison."

17. "Do what my sister Nacha recommends…that you go to Mexico with her. That way you don't have to go to the war,"

tras sin el gobierno buscandome." [18]

"Entonces vete con los parientes de tu papá. Ellos tienen dinero," [19] suggests his mother.

"No. No. No. Con esa gente no se va ningunos de mis hijos. Esos parientes de primero estaban con la revolución, y luego se hicieron al lado del gobierno y contra de mi jefe, Pancho Villa. Prefiero que maten a mi hijo en Viet Nam de que le vaya ver las carotas a esos traidores," [20] says Machete's father with condemnation.

Machete knows that his father does not wish him dead because he understands how much his father hates that side of the family.

"Mire hijo, pongase muy trucha y tenga tanates y lo demas que pase es solo para Dios que diga," [21] advises his father when the mother is out of listening range.

"Sí, apá. Ama me voy a bañar para listarme para irme." [22]

When Machete returns to the kitchen he is "strack," as soldiers say. His boots are spit-shined, his brass sparkles and his uniform is dry cleaned.

"Sientate hijo a comer tu almuerzo," [23] says his mother holding back tears.

---

18. "Mom, like I told your earlier, poor aunt Nacha is barley making it, and anyway there isn't any work over there. All the people come to work over here. And if I go to Mexico I won't be able to return because the government will be looking for me."
19. "Then go with your fathers relatives. They have money," suggest his mother.
20. "No. No. No. None of my sons will go with those people. Those people started out fighting for the Revolution and then they went against my chief Poncho Villa. I prefer that they kill my son in Viet Nam than he go and see those traitor's faces," says his father with condemnation.
21. "Look son, be smart have balls and what ever happens after that is for God to say,"
22. "Yes Dad. Mom I'm going to take a shower to get ready to leave."
23. "Sit down and eat your breakfast son,"

Machete can not stand to see his mother cry, so he gulps down his breakfast of chorizo, eggs and tortillas as quickly as he can. When he finishes, he asks his father to give him a ride to Chuco's house. He has asked them not to take him to the airport because he knows it would be an emotional strain on his mother. He gets up from the table, hugs his crying mother good-bye and leaves through the back door.

When they reach Chuco's house, Machete shakes his father's hand and gets off the car. "Buena suerte hijo, y acuerdese: Tenga tanates y pongase trucha y lo demas está en las manos de Dios," [24] his father tells him as he drives away.

---

24. "Good luck son. Remember, be smart, have balls and the rest is in God's hands,"

Episode IV
Last Kiss

Chuco wakes up in a cold cell. His body aches from the beating he received and can barely move. He rotates his tongue inside his mouth and feels one of his front teeth missing. What a night, que pinche noche,[1] he reflects. Man! Now I know how grandpa feels when he gets up in the morning. He manages to slowly get up to the cell door and call out, "Get me out of here! I need to catch a plane to Viet Nam. Get me out of here!"

"What's all the ruckus about?" asks a thin policeman with a cigarette dangling from his mouth.

"I've got to catch a plane to Viet Nam in a couple of hours."

"Bullshit," says the policeman.

"No shit, man. Just let me call my brother and he'll tell you."

"Okay, but you'd better be telling the truth or you're going to be up shit creek."

Chuco is let out of the cell and slowly walks to the booking room and calls home. His brother, The Gang, answers the phone and says, "Where you been, chili bean? It's five o'clock and your plane leaves at seven."

"I know, but Pichon and his puto friends kicked my ass last night and I'm here in jail. Go pick up Machete and Ese and come over to see if you can get me out. Don't forget to bring my duffel bag and uniform. Let me talk to dad. Mire apá aquí estoy en la carcel porque me brincaron unos vatos. Pero hice como usted nos enseño, no comensé el pleito pero no corrí tampoco.[2] I don't want mom to see me like this

1. What a fucking night.
2. "Look dad, I'm here in jail because some guys jumped on me. I did like you
   taught us; I didn't start the fight but I didn't run either.

so tell her I'll see her in a year?"

Just as Chuco hangs up, Junior walks in and says, "Well, if it isn't our hero. Who were you calling?"

"My brother. He's coming over here to see if he can bail me out."

"There's no need for that, Poncho, I'm going to be a nice guy and let you out. I wouldn't want you to miss an opportunity to get your ass killed. As a matter of fact, I wish they would take all you niggers and greasers so you can kill one another with all those gooks. And if you do get your greasy ass killed, I'm going to lead your funeral parade free of charge. Get him his things and get him the hell out of here," he orders the other policeman.

Chuco doesn't say anything as he is lead out, but stares wickedly at Junior. On the sidewalk outside the jail, the sun introduces itself with purple and orange red streaked hues. Chuco stares at the sunrise and wonders if the sun will look the same in Viet Nam.

As Chuco stares at the sunrise, The Gang drives up in a brown 1957 two-door Ford Fairlane with white button-tuck Tijuana custom upholstery. Chuco quickly jumps in the back seat of the car.

"Hijole, que chingados te pasó a ti.[3] It looks like you ran into the Tasmanian Devil. Man, your lips are bigger than a mayate's,"[4] says The Gang.

"It was those assholes, Pichon and his camaradas. Pichon got pissed off because I was with Sleepy-Eyes."

"As I told you before son, don't lose your head over a piece of tail," teases Machete.

"Don't call me son. I've told you about that shit before," says Chuco in anger.

Machete laughs because he knows how to get Chuco riled.

---

3. "What the fuck happened to you.
4. june bug (a black),"

"Let's go find Pichon and go kick the fuck out of him," says The Gang.

"I don't think that's a good idea—look who's behind us," says Machete.

The Gang looks into the rear-view and mirror and says, "It's that asshole, Puñetas."

"Forget that punk. Let's go pick up Ese and get the hell out of Dodge. I'll settle with Pichon when I get back," says Chuco.

They reach Chanclas' house and The Gang honks the horn. He waits a few seconds and honks again.

"I don't think he's coming out. I'll go in and get his ass out," says Machete. He walks into the dilapidated wooden house with a creaky porch. The door is slightly open and Machete walks in. He is familiar with the house because they have partied here nearly every night for the last month. He goes to the refrigerator, grabs a bottle of beer and opens it with an opener. He takes a drink of beer and goes to the bedroom.

Ese, in his underwear, is laying face down and has his right arm and leg on Chanclas. Machete takes his comb out and slowly runs the teeth against the sole of Ese's feet. Ese reacts with an annoying grunt. "Get the fuck up, trooper," yells Machete in his best drill sergeant act. "We've got a job to do."

"What, what the fuck...where we going?" asks Ese, startled and dumfounded.

"Viet Nam, boy. We've got some gooks to kill. Get your shit together and let's go. Move it...move it...maggot. Quickly, quickly," he barks. "We'll be waiting for you outside."

Machete leaves the room, takes a six-pack of beer out of the refrigerator and walks to the car. He opens a beer, hands it to Chuco and tells him, "You need this, fella."

Chuco grabs the beer and drinks it from the right side of his mouth because the other side is too swollen to drink from.

"Here comes Puñetas again," says The Gang as the policeman slowly drives by. "He ain't going to leave you guys alone until you leave. Where in the hell is that stupid Ese?"

"There he is," says Machete as they see Ese on the porch, trying to tuck his shirt in as Chanclas is grabbing on to him saying, "Come on, baby, give me one more last kiss, just one more."

"Not now, can't you see all the guys are watching and laughing?"

The Gang yells out, "Just one more, it ain't going to kill you."

Chuco puts his arms around his torso and says, "Tell him to stop because the laughing is hurting my face and ribs."

"Dale un pinche kiss y vamonos a la verga," [5] says Machete.

Ese does and runs to the car and complains as he gets in, "Boy, that girl sure has bad breath."

"Ese, Ese, you forgot the pelos," [6] calls out Chanclas.

"Oh, yeah," says Ese, as he darts back out of the car and takes the plastic bag from Chanclas' hand. He puts it in his pocket and gratefully tells her, "Gracias, mujer." [7]

"Hijo, that was just like in the movies. You ought to be a movie star. What's in the bag, goose?" asks The Gang.

"Candy...Magic Candy!" replies Ese. "Give me a ride to my mom's house so I can shower and change into my uniform."

"We ain't got no time for all that. We've got just enough time to make it to the airport after you pick up your stuff," says The Gang.

They arrive at Ese's house and he dashes inside. His mother and little sister are sitting in the living room listening to the radio.

"Buenos dias, amá. [8] I'm sorry I didn't come home last night...but

---

5. "Give her a fucking kiss and let's get the fuck out of here,"
6. hairs,"
7. "Thank you woman."
8. "Good morning mom.

I'm late and I've got to go. I just came to pick up my stuff." He goes to the bedroom, grabs his duffel bag and bids his mother and sister farewell. He does this with little ceremony, but with tenderness, and tells her as he leaves out the door, "Hay nos vemos en un año amá."

"Sí mijo, cuidate," [9] says his mother, her face enveloped with concealed pain.

Ranita is just tall enough to peer over the window ledge. Her eyes are glossy with tears as she somberly waves to Ese and gently whispers, "Adios, mi hermanito." [10]

The roosters crow obstreperously and can be heard throughout the barrio. They seem to know that the homeboys are on their way to a remarkable and portentous adventure.

"Step on it, Gang, or we'll be late," says Ese as he gets in the car. "Holy shit, what happened to you!" says Ese, noticing Chuco for the first time. "Don't tell me…it was Pichon and them dudes, Wolfdaddy and Craterface. Like they say…"

"Yeah, yeah I know: 'never lose your head over a piece of tail.' If I hear that one more time, I'm going to knock one of you donkeys in the head. Gangster, why don't you stop at the river store to buy some beer? Because, like my carnal, Huesos, told us, we'll be out in the bush for weeks at a time and won't have any beer or anything else. So we'd better party while we can."

The Gang stops at the store and parks next to a hippie van painted with red, green, orange and purple psychedelic colors and designs.

"Go fetch the beer, boy," Machete orders Chuco.

"I told you for the last time, don't call me boy." angrily answers Chuco.

"Son of a bitch. Look at that hippie ruca next to the van. Hija de su

---

9. "I'll see you in a year mom. "Yes son, take care,"
10. "Good-bye, my little brother."

pinche madre.[11] Look at the culo[12] she's got. Está más buenota que la chingada,"[13] says Machete with lust, as he stares at a tall, long-haired blond with tight hip-hugger pants on.

Just as he finishes his sentence, the blond turns around and looks toward them.

"It's a hippie vato," declares The Gang.

"Boy, you ain't lying, and he's an ugly son of a bitch. Look at the the beard on that asshole," says Ese.

Machete turns red with embarrassment and knows it will be a while before he will live his mistake down.

At the airport, the soldiers quickly change into their military uniforms. They say their good-byes to The Gang and are just able to board the plane before it takes off. After deplaning in San Francisco, the three head for the USO lounge. At the lounge they help themselves to doughnuts, coffee and milk, and sit down at one of the many card tables. The lounge is full of commuting servicemen; a muffled clamor fills the room.

"What do you think they're going to do to us when we report two weeks late?" asks Ese as he sips his coffee.

"My brother Huesos says they ain't going to do nothing to us because the army would rather have us out in the bush than in jail," answers Chuco.

"Something tells me that we shouldn't go," says Machete.

"What the fuck else we going to do—go to Canada? We don't got nobody over there and we don't got no money. What are we going to do, call up our moms and tell them to send us some money because we're going to desert? Or are we going to go to Mexico? Shit, people are so poor over there that they come up this way just to work. We'd

11. What a bitch.
12. ass
13. She's finer than fuck,"

never survive over there," assures Ese.

"Here come the MPs," warns Chuco. "And they're coming our way."

Two military police with starched uniforms and spit-shined boots walk directly to their table. "Where's your orders?" asks one of the MPs intimidatingly.

Ese, who enjoys lying, bemusing and wisecracking to authority, especially the police, answers, "They're in our duffel bags, which are on our plane that has been delayed."

"Well, I can see you guys are just out of training, so from now on, always hand carry your orders," advises one of the MPs. "Why are you wearing your raincoat inside the terminal?" he asks Ese.

"It's because I got too fat on my leave from eating too much chorizo, beans and tortillas, and my pants won't buckle," says Ese as he unbuttons his raincoat and shows him a large safety pin holding his pants up. The MPs chuckle and leave. Ese gloats for once again disarming a menacing authority with his wit and sense of humor. "Boy! I sure do hate those candy-ass Military Pigs. They're just like army lifers and flies; they eat shit and bother people."

They wait a few minutes for the MPs to leave so that they can retrieve their duffel bags at the entrance of the lounge. After doing so, they wait outside the terminal and wait for a bus to take them to the Oakland Army Terminal. As they wait, a dark blue 63 super sport Chevy Impala parks in front of them. Two Chicano soldiers get off of the car. Both are indios, except that one is short and the other tall. The tall one has a mean scar across his left cheek. They both have tiny lacerations on their hands given to them by thorns and elephant grass in their struggle with the jungle.

Instantly, Chuco, Ese and Machete recognize the First Cavalry patch on their right shoulders which indicates they are Viet Nam veterans.

They know this because of the army's tradition to use a collage of patches and insignias to represent a soldier's history and accomplishments. They are infantry and veterans of war with their unit's insignia on their right shoulder, a blue braid around their left shoulder and a combat badge on their chest. But then again, these trinkets can be bought by anyone for a few cents at the Post Exchange. They recognize by their demeanor and physical appearance that these soldiers don't need any ornaments to tell where they just came from.

"You vatos going to Nam?" asks the tall soldier, walking toward the trunk and in between the car and sidewalk.

"Yeah. We're going to the Oakland Army Terminal," answers Machete.

"You guys need a ride?" asks the short soldier.

"Sure, we could use one," says Machete.

"You vatos wait a minute while we get our bags out of the car, and you can hitch a ride with my brother Wilo. We're from Richmond and that's on his way home. Our orders are for Fort Polk, Louisiana and we're going to push troops."

Wilo, a thin teenager with a tattoo of the wicked cross between his thumb and index finger, approaches Machete and shakes his hand.

"I'm Machete and this is Ese and Chuco."

"Órale, carnales,"[14] says Wilo as he shakes Ese's and Chuco's hand.

"Traemos, prisa[15] and we've got to split. Remember to keep your asses down, and when you're under attack, keep firing back or else those assholes will be on your cases and fuck you up," warns the tall soldier as he and the short soldier leave with their duffel bags on their shoulders.

---

14. "All right brothers,"
15. "We're in a hurry

EPISODE V
Purple Haze

They leave the airport and drive onto the freeway. "You vatos want to take a cruise around San Pancho[1] before I take you to Oakland?" asks Wilo. "I don't go there too often."

"Sounds like a good idea to me," says Machete.

"Sure, a toda madre," [2] agrees Chuco. "I want to see some of those hippie rucas."

"Me too. But I don't like the kind that Machete likes," says Ese as he and Chuco bust out laughing.

"Do you want to go to Chinatown first?" asks Wilo.

"Hell no. We're going to see a lot of those bastards in Viet Nam," answers Machete.

"Let's go to Haight Ashbury and check out the stupid hippies and peace creeps," says Ese.

"O.K., the next turnoff will take us to the Haight," says Wilo.

After they exit the freeway, Ese asks Wilo to stop at a liquor store. Ese gets off and brings back a bag of peanuts and a case of beer.

"Shit, you vatos really like to party, huh?" says Wilo.

"Fucking-a-right, carnal," says Ese, as he passes everyone a beer.

Chuco is still smarting from his wounds. He takes a drink of beer and grimaces and says, "Hijo de su…[3] the first drink is the hardest one." He takes another drink and finishes the beer in one gulp. "Hora si, me siento más de aquellas," [4] he says as he closes his eyes and lies limp. He envisions himself laying in a field of tall grass. A mellifluous

---

1. Frisco
2. sounds bitching
3. "Son of a gun…
4. "I feel a lot better now,"

female voice repeats over and over, "Te quiero...I quiero you...Te quiero un chingo[5]...I love you."

"Wake up, stupid. You think you're sleeping beauty, ¿o qué?"[6] rudely says Machete as he nudges Chuco. "We're here with the hippie putos."

"We'll just cruise a little while to see what's happening here. If we see something we like, we'll stop and get off," says Wilo. The streets are brimming with flower children. Females are dressed in long skirts with jubilant floral patterns. Jangling bracelets on their wrists, with bright ring-filled hands and brilliant beads around their necks give them a festive appearance. The men are dressed in loose fitting shirts with many of the same patterns and colors the women wear. They wear their bell bottom pants tight. Their beards generate a prophet-like aura.

"Boy, I hate these punk hippies," says Machete with rancor. "They ain't worth a fuck. And most of them are communist. You know, these assholes actually raise the Vietnamese communist flag. They ought to be shot."

"I bet you their parents have feria.[7] I don't like people who act poor but who really have money. As soon as they get tired of being poor, they just go home to mama and papa and they're not poor anymore. They're phony. But I guess there might be a few sincere ones," says Ese.

"Me importa pito si son comunistas o ricos.[8] I don't like them because they're asshole gabachos[9] and they act like they're real chingones," says Chuco with nonchalant animosity.

Wilo abruptly says, "I'm going to park the car because I just saw a headshop. I need to get me a waterpipe." He parks the car close to

5. "I love you...I love you...I love you a lot...
6. or what,"
7. dough (money)
8. "I don't give a shit if they're communist or rich.
9. whites

the headshop and asks, "You vatos going to get off?"

"Nel, I don't think so, eh. It's probably better not to get off with our uniforms on," says Ese with precaution.

"It's not that we are scared of them, but there are too many of them for us to fight," adds Machete. "We'll just sit here, drink beer, and watch the bitches go by."

"We know the kind of hippies you like," says Chuco as he and Ese burst out laughing.

"I'll be back in a few minutes," says Wilo.

Once again, Chuco falls into a lull. The same tranquil voice says, "Te quiero...I quiero you...Te quiero un chingo...I love you."

Ese and Machete quietly drink beer as they watch the hippies pass by. Two hippies, one black and the other white, stop to talk to them from the curb. They try to sell them marijuana.

"You want to buy some weed, man?" says the white hippie in a soft narcotic voice.

"What you got?" asks Ese.

"We got some Panama Red," says the black hippie, a Jimi Hendrix look alike.

"How much?," asks Ese.

"Ten dollars a lid," answers the black hippie.

"Naw, that's too much money," says Ese, knowing well that it is a fair price.

"What do you mean too much?" says the black hippie in a sour note.

"Fuck you, man," says Machete in his usual pugnacious manner when he doesn't like someone.

"Cool it, man," says the white hippie. "There isn't any reason to get angry. We are all children of the sun. Peace, man," he says with his eyes sparkling like blue jello. "You guys want to buy some far out acid man? We got orange sunshine and purple haze."

Hearing the voices, Chuco recovers from his interlude. The first thing he sees is the black hippie. "It's Jimi Hendrix," says Chuco. "Hey, Jimi, sing us a song. Play, 'Purple Haze'; that's my favorite."

"What's wrong with this fool?" says the black hippie tartly. Ignoring Chuco he continues, "You want to buy any of this good shit or not? We ain't got time to be jiving with you."

"What's the problem?," says Wilo as he gets in the car.

"Man, you are some jive motherfuckers," says the black hippie insultingly.

"Wilo, ponte trucha porque cuando te diga, nos vamos de volada porque le voy a rebatar la bolsa," [10] says Machete. "O.K., O.K man, let's see what you got. The white hippie brings out a bag of acid and one of marijuana. As soon as he does, Machete grabs both of them and tells Wilo, "Vamonos a la chingada. Dale gas." [11]

Wilo zips out of the parking space. The black hippie is quick to react. He holds on to the door handle and yells out, "You motherfucking Meskins!"

"Go faster," says Machete. The black hippie is adamant and holds on to the door handle until Machete burns the hand with a lit cigarette. The black hippie falls to the ground, shouting and cursing.

They all laugh as they drive away. Ese says, "Those clowns thought they were going to get over on us just because we're from a small town. It's about time we go to Viet Nam, don't you think?"

"Chale, let's go to North Beach and check out the rucas," says Chuco. "What do you think, Wilo?"

"Sounds de aquellas to me. Vamos," [12] he answers.

"Wow, look at the weed. It's Panama red. Look at the acid," says Ese

---

10. Wilo be alert because when I tell you to split, I'm going to grab the bag.
11. "Let's get the fuck out of here. Punch the gas."
12. good to me. Let's go,"

as he opens the second bag. "What do you want Wilo, some purple haze or some orange sunshine?"

"Dame[13] some sunshine."

"Para mi también," [14] says Chuco.

"Here you go. One for you, and one for you," Ese tells them as he hands them the acid. "Aqual quieres tu,[15] Machete?" Ese asks.

"I don't take any of that communist hippie shit," answers Machete.

"Just for that, you don't get any, pinche culo. I'll take the haze because I don't want to get silly like Chuco," says Ese as he tilts his head and places the acid in his mouth like he is receiving communion. "Since you're going to punk out, why don't you fill the water pipe with grifa?" [16]

"Now that's a different story," says Machete, smiling and grabbing the waterpipe. He fills it with marijuana. They all take turns smoking from the waterpipe. The narcotic effect of the marijuana takes hold and no one talks for a while. Wilo gets lost and ends up in the Mission District. From there, they end up on Market Street and two hours later, they find North Beach.

"Mira a todas las luces.[17] It's fantastic," says Chuco. Neon lights bombard his senses and he sees sounds of music emanating in vivid colors. The passing cars are slowly transformed into horse-drawn wagons, driven by old Italian men eating pizza pies. "Find a place to park Wilo. We got to get off." Wilo finds a parking space and they walk to North Beach.

Outside the topless nightclubs are women enticing men to step into the clubs. Chuco sees the faces of the women melting like wax dummies under ardent heat. It doesn't frighten him because he knows it's

13. "Give me
14. "For me too,
15. "Which do you want,
16. marijuana
17. "Look at all the lights.

only the acid's effect on him.

"Hijo de la chingada.[18] Look at all these beautiful babes," says Ese with glee. He blows kisses to the women. "Que buenas estan mamasotas," [19] he tells them.

Finally, they reach the club where Carol Doda works. They gather around to see her picture in front of the club. "Wow, look at the chichis[20] on this whore. Man, they're the biggest knockers I've ever seen," says Chuco in astonishment.

"How much is it to go in?" Machete asks the barker.

"Five dollars cover and two drink minimum. That comes out to twelve dollars each." Without hesitation, they pay and walk into the club. They are in luck and are able to get a table close to the stage. The music is blaring but abruptly stops when the MC approaches the stage.

"Bring on Carol. Bring on Carol," Ese yells.

"She'll be out in a little while there, soldier boy," answers the MC "But first, we have the honor of having Bobby Freeman here with us tonight. So give a big round of applause to Bobby Freeman and "The Swim.""

"All-right. All-right, Bobby!" yells Ese.

Bobby Freeman first sings some of his lesser known songs until he eventually sings his biggest hit, "The Swim." While Bobby sings and does the swim, Ese gets up from the table and also does the swim. A muscular bouncer walks up to Ese and tells him, "Look soldier boy, you've got to sit down and quit dancing or else you're going to have to leave."

"Sure man. I'm not doing anything wrong."

"You heard what I said," forewarns the bouncer.

18. Son of a whore.
19. "You're some fine mamas,"
20. tits

After Bobby Freeman does his routine, Carol Doda comes on. Chuco and Machete whistle loudly and the audience becomes rambunctious. Ese gets up and tries to get close to Carol. The bouncer goes up to Ese and tells him, "Look soldier boy, I'm telling you for the last time to sit down. You keep misbehaving and we're going to eighty-six you."

"Right, O.K. man, I'll sit down," concedes Ese, knowing well he is out of his element. After a couple of numbers, Carol begins to take off her blouse. Ese loses control and tries to get close to her again.

The bouncer, followed by two other bouncers, comes up behind Ese, grabs him from his collar and belt buckle, and escorts him out. Ese's comrades follow suit, but don't interfere, knowing that if they do, it will produce negative results.

Ese's face is flushed with rage. He is powerless to retaliate against his bigger and stronger opponent. The bouncer takes him to the door and releases him. Swiftly, Ese turns around and pokes the bouncer in the eye with his thumb. The bouncer grabs his eye in pain, and then Ese kicks him in the shins. He runs away with the rest of his cohorts running behind him. They laugh all the way to the car.

"You should've seen that punk-dago-wop-motherfucker's face when I poked him in the eye. Then when I kicked him in the shin, he didn't know whether to grab his face or his shin. That son-of-a-bitch was calling me a greaser and spic when he had a hold of me. Let's get the flock out of here. We've got to go to Viet Nam."

EPISODE VI
Feathered Metal Eagle

When they reach the Bay Bridge, Machete fills the waterpipe with marijuana. They smoke up a blast as they cross the bridge. Ese takes a giant drag and says, after he blows the smoke out the window, "We're blessing the bridge."

They arrive at the gate of the base and obtain permission to enter. "We've got to go to building B134. I know where it's at," says Wilo. "That's where I left my brother and primo when they were going to Viet Nam." Wilo drives them to the building. The duffel bags are unloaded and Wilo bids them farewell.

"Good luck," says Machete to Wilo.

"Man, I'm still fucked up," says Ese, as he rubs his eyes and tries to focus on Wilo driving away.

"What time is it?" asks Chuco.

"It's twenty-four hundred hours," says Machete.

"Shit ese, you're starting to sound like a lifer," says Ese. "Time sure has gone by fast."

"¿Por qué sera?" [1] says Machete.

"It must be the acid, huh?" asks Ese naively.

"No stupid, it was the cokes."

"Vamos a entrar,[2] and see what they tell us," says Chuco.

They proceed into a building and walk directly to a bespectacled specialist fourth-class. Several soldiers sit on benches waiting to be assigned sleeping quarters.

"Where are your orders?" asks the clerk.

---

1. "I wonder why?"
2. "Let's go in,

41

Man, this is a tired honkie, thinks Ese, as he notices the dandruff on the clerk's thick eyebrows.

They give him their orders. He scans the papers and finally says, "You soldiers are AWOL twenty-nine days. One more day and you'll be classified deserters. This is serious," he says as he picks a up a telephone. "Hello, I need some MPs. I've got three soldiers here who are AWOL 29 days. You wait here, I'm going down the hall to call the officer of the day," says the clerk, scurrying down the hall with easy-going carelessness.

An officer and an asshole, thinks Ese.

Shortly, the clerk returns with a captain with a stoic demeanor. "Ten-hut!" yells the specialist. Ese, Chuco and Machete promptly stand at attention. "So you soldiers are AWOL?" says the captain. "Why are you men AWOL?"

"Because we wanted to have a good time, sir," answers Machete. "But we're ready to leave now, sir."

"How gracious of you, private. Do you think you men make the rules? If there wasn't a war going on, I'd have you guys in the stockade," he answers in a gruff voice. "The war is heating up and we need all the infantry we can muster. So I'm going to give you soldiers a break and send you out on the first plane I can. What time is the next flight out?" he asks the specialist.

"In four hours, sir."

"Make sure these jay-birds are on it."

"We can't do that, sir, because the manifest is complete. Besides the next orientation is not until tomorrow."

"The hell with the orientation. Take some clerks or cooks off the manifest and put these infantry soldiers on the plane."

"Yes sir," obeys the clerk. "Here are your orders," he tells them as he stretches out his arm to give them their papers. Chuco sees the hair on the specialist's arms grow like cactus thorns with minute beetle heads at the end, saying in loud whispers, like porky pig, "And…and that's all folks." It's only the acid, he deduces.

After they finish processing three hours later, the effects of the alcohol and marijuana have worn off, but not the acid. They have been issued jungle fatigues and boots and are jiving one another on how they look.

"You look like a double-lipped dog with fatigues on," Ese tells Machete.

"No le creas,[3] Machete. You look more like Peter Lorre, only darker," says Chuco.

"Fuck both of you. You're acting like idiots with all that stupid acid you took."

"Jesus. What's all those blue spots doing on your face," says Ese as he touches Machete's forehead.

"There ain't no spots, baboso,"[4] says Machete slapping Ese's hand from his forehead.

"Wow! Look at his boots; they sure are small," says Ese.

"That's because he has hoofs like Eddie Munster. Haven't you ever wondered why he runs like a billy goat?" says Chuco as he laughs.

"No esten chingando babosos.[5] Let's go to the barracks they told us to go to," says Machete.

"Let's go get something to eat first. I haven't had anything to eat since yesterday. The specialist said the mess hall is to the right of this building," says Chuco as he leads them out of the building.

They find the mess hall full of soldiers and, regardless of the height, weight and race of the soldiers, they all look the same. "How do you want your steak and eggs?" asks a cook with a huge potbelly hanging

3. "Don't believe him,

4. idiot,"

5. "Don't be fucking around idiots.

over his belt.

"What?" asks Ese in disbelief.

"You heard what I said, maggot."

"I'll have the eggs over-easy and the steak well-done. I can't believe this," Ese tells Machete. "All we had in training was powdered eggs and shit on the shingle." They fill their tray with eggs, steaks, toast and pancakes. After eating, they go to the barracks that they are assigned to. Ese and Chuco are unable to sleep because of the acid. While Chuco and Ese play poker with other soldiers, Machete finds a bunk and falls sleeps.

Machete is awakened by a slim, yet powerfully built sergeant shouting, "All right all you worthless maggots, formation…on the double, on the double. We ain't got no time for lolly-gagging." Machete gathers himself and puts on his right boot. "What the fuck," he says. "It smells like piss. Somebody pissed in my boot." Ese and Chuco can't help but laugh.

I'll get those fuckers later, vows Machete as he runs out of the building with his right boot sloshing with urine.

After everyone's name is called out, they are loaded on a bus for the forty mile trip to Travis Air Force Base. As they leave Oakland, a slumbering morning arrives with a yawning peace.

At Travis, the bus taxies directly to the awaiting Flying Tiger Airline jet. When the bus stops, the sergeant yells again, "Move it. Move it, maggots, we've got to get you to Viet Nam." The soldiers are trained to instantly obey commands and fall out a few meters from the jet plane. A thick fog accompanied by a chilling breeze surrounds the airfield. The soldiers suffer because the jungle fatigues do not protect them against the cold.

Two hours later, the fog lifts and the soldiers are allowed to board the plane. Once seated near the rear of the plane, Ese scans the plane as the last effects of the acid allow him to identify the soldiers who are going to die in Viet Nam; they are the ones dressed in flag-draped coffins. He doesn't dare to turn and look at Chuco or Machete for fear of them also dressed in flag-draped coffins. And he certainly doesn't look in the window to his right to see his reflection.

A synthetic voice comes over the intercom, "This is the captain speaking. Welcome on board flight X1314 to Bien Hoa airport in the Republic of South Viet Nam. Our flight is scheduled to stop at Honolulu, Hawaii and then re-fuel at Anderson Air Base, Guam. As soon as the stewardesses give you instructions on emergencies, we will be on our way. If you need anything, ask one of the stewardesses and she will assist you. Have a pleasant flight."

"M'am," Chuco politely asks a passing stewardess with mechanical, crystal blue eyes. "Can I have a pillow?"

"I don't know, can you?" she answers in a poisonous tone.

"All I want is a pillow," says Chuco again.

"Well get it yourself, you piece of barbecue shit," she answers with rancor.

"Fuck you, puta," [6] says Chuco with controlled anger.

Machete laughs and tells Chuco, "Save it for the fight, killer."

Finally, the plane takes off like a giant silver eagle reaching for eternity. Most of the soldiers fall asleep and the rest are in quiet contemplation. Ese has his recurring dream. He wakes up sweating. Pain and loneliness taunt his soul and he is unable to fall asleep again.

Three hours later, the feathered metal eagle untucks its wheeled talons, and, as if by wizardry, touches the runway. The passengers deplane and are allowed to wait on the top deck bar of the airport.

---

6. whore

"Hijola[7] feel the breeze," says Machete with as he sits down. "I could stay here forever."

"Forget it, Machete, we already went through that," says Ese matter-of-factly.

"Look at all these gabacho[8] tourists. How come we got to be going to Viet Nam in order to be here?" asks Machete.

"Olvidate de Acapulco.[9] We ain't got much of a choice now," says Ese.

"Simon,[10] fuck that noise. We've already decided. Let's get something to drink," says Chuco as he gets up in his usual assertive stride toward the bar. The one hour lay-over passes quickly but not before most of the soldiers are feeling the proverbial "little pain" from the alcohol consumed.

---

7. "Wow,
8. white man
9. "Forget about it
10. "Yeah,

EPISODE VII
Viet Nam

The passengers are rudely awakened by the intercom, "Please extinguish your cigarettes, fasten your seat belts and bring your seats to an upright position. For those of you that have been asleep, we have flown straight through from Hawaii because there was typhoon damage to the runway in Guam. Welcome to the Republic of Viet Nam."

The reality of finally getting to Viet Nam is met by reluctant relief by most of the soldiers. As they deplane, the hot air hits them like a hot fan and Chuco says, "Está haciendo más calor que la chingada." [1]

They all walk towards the terminal in single file. Soldiers boarding the plane for the States pass them by. "Look at those lucky suckers. They already get to go home. Look at that little mayatio," [2] points Ese. "He's drunker than shit. I wish I had some of the same of whatever he had."

"Uptight. Uptight," yells the little soldier. "Uptight. Uptight. That's right, motherfuckers," he screams to the incoming soldiers, "You'd better tighten up and not lighten up…or else Charlie Cong is going to tighten you up." He laughs and continues, "Uptight. Uptight. Motherfuckers. And you all going to die."

From the airport, they are loaded on cattle trucks to the replacement station. When they arrive, a sergeant first-class greets them with less harassment than previous sergeants. However, his attitude is more stoic and detached. Once the soldiers are in formation he says, "Listen up. As I call your names, fall out to my left." He calls a dozen names which include Ese, Chuco and Machete. "You people are to report to the mess hall for kitchen police."

---

1. "It's hotter than hell."
2. black,"

"Just our luck," says Machete, "We're going to wash pots and pans and peel potatoes." After 14 hours of K.P., they are allowed to sleep for six hours before they are called back for duty. On the third day, while peeling potatoes, they are told to fall out in front of the barracks.

The air is muggy and humid as the sergeant orders the troops to attention. Ese is included in the first set of names bawled out. "All of you soldiers are going to the First Infantry Division in Di An. Get in the trucks and move out," he orders. Ese heads for the truck, looks back toward Chuco and Machete and gives them a shit-eating grin.

Machete's name is called in the next round and he is assigned to the Americal Division. His group will be flown to their northern destination several hundred miles away. He doesn't bother to look toward Chuco as he boards the truck.

The last group of soldiers named includes Chuco. "You people are going to the Ninth Infantry in the Mekong Delta in Dong Tam." They are also loaded on cattle trucks.

EPISODE VIII
Chuco's Unit

Chuco and his group are taken to Dong Tam, a three-hour ride from the reception station. Along the way, he notices the poverty and hostility of the people. He sees that many of the people dress in clothes like Mexicans during the Revolution of 1910, only these clothes are black instead of white. In training, he had been told that the enemy, the South Vietnamese guerillas called Viet Cong by the U.S. military, wore black pajamas. He thinks everybody must be the enemy because everyone is wearing black pajamas.

At one point along the way, the truck has to slow down because some water buffalos are blocking the road. Before the truck can come to a complete stop, a shot rings out and a bullet shatters the windshield. Instinctively, the soldiers jump off the truck and head for cover. Chuco doesn't know how to react, and once off of the truck, he runs around the truck and winds up where he started. To Chuco's relief, everyone is so busy looking for cover that they didn't notice what he did. After a few minutes, the word is given that it is clear to board the truck. Chuco feels silly, but since no one saw him run around the truck, it doesn't matter. He knows he has just learned a good lesson. He also wishes they would have issued them their weapons.

As the truck pulls out, small children run behind the truck asking for candy or food. Some of the soldiers are bothered by the kids, while others are indifferent. A few give them C-ration candies. Chuco teases one of the kids and holds candy just far enough for the kid not to be able to reach it. As the truck goes faster, the kid tries to keep up and reach for the candy. The truck cannot go very fast because of all the people on the road The kid is able to keep up for a kilometer until Chuco has teased him enough, and gives him the candy.

They finally arrive at the Ninth Infantry Division headquarters in Dong Tam. Again, they are told to fall out, and Chuco is picked for K.P. I bet you that stupid Ese is kicking back somewhere hiding from the sergeants, thinks Chuco. He reports to the mess hall and is assigned to peel potatoes. He joins two other Chicanos sitting around a small pot of unpeeled potatoes and a larger one with peeled potatoes.

One of the soldiers asks Chuco as he sits down, "What's your name, ese? ¿De dónde eres?"

"Soy de Califas, y me dicen Chuco," [1] answers Chuco in a serious tone.

"Yo soy Ro-Ro y este vato es la Liebre. [2] Liebre looks just as his name implies; a long thin face, slender body with large jack rabbit ears. Ro-Ro is well-built and fancies himself an Elvis Presley look alike.

"I hope you'll be in our platoon. We're all Chicanos y no la llevamos a toda madre. [3] Right, Ro-Ro?"

"Sirol. [4] We're all carnales, except sometimes we fight each other," answers Ro-Ro mirthfully. "That's all the papas to peel. Vamos al cuarto de atrás a fumarnos un leño." [5]

Ro-Ro leads them to a dark storage room. When Liebre closes the door behind him, his eyes sparkle like jack-rabbit eyes. Ro-Ro lights up an opium-laced marijuana cigarette and takes a healthy drag. Then he hands it to Chuco. "Cuidate moro; [6] this grifa has opium," warns Ro-Ro.

Chuco also inhales deeply and, in a nanosecond, the opium ignites

---

1. Where you from?" "I'm from California and they call me Chuco,"
2. I'm Ro-Ro and they call this guy Jack-Rabbit.
3. And we all get along fine.
4. "Yeah.
5. Let's go to the back room and smoke some a joint."
6. "Be careful kid;

a harmonious feeling. Suddenly, the door opens.

"Órale pinche putos.[7] I've been looking for you assholes," says a diminutive soldier with a bottle of tequila in his left hand.

"It's Wino, says Ro-Ro. "¿Qué traes, loco cabron?"[8]

"Is this the new vato?"

"Simón," answers Ro-Ro.

"He's in our platoon. What happened to you vatos last night? I heard que le dieron en la madre a un gabacho,"[9] says Wino.

"Yeah, me and Liebre went into this bar outside the gate and it was full of gringos. After a while, one of those big-headed ex-football player assholes begins to fuck with us. You know, the kind that are big chicken shits out in the bush. He wouldn't leave us alone until Liebre follows him to the latrine and cuts his ass."

"Me lo chingue,"[10] says Liebre smiling. "I wanted to know what he had for lunch."

"Then we ran to that crazy mama-san's house and hid out until this morning. We had some fun with some gookas.[11] The captain himself saw us coming in late this morning and gave us K.P. He took us to his office and told us that if it were up to him, he'd court-martial us. But instead, he wouldn't because it's more punishment to be out in the field. I never liked that son-of-a-bitch. And he doesn't like me. One time, when I was in his office for being AWOL, he told me that Mexicans are nothing but niggers with straight hair and gooks with round eyes. Then the puto took my sergeant stripes from me," says Ro-Ro.

"Forget it. They won't catch you for fucking up the gabacho because we're moving out in a couple of hours. No te aguites. Andale, dejate

---

7. "What's happening motherfuckers
8. What's up you crazy fucker?
9. that you fucked up a white boy,"
10. "I messed him up,"
11. Vietnamese women

caer un pajualajo de tequila," [12] says Wino, handing the bottle of tequila to Ro-Ro.

Ro-Ro takes a huge swig of tequila and passes the bottle to Liebre. When Chuco takes a drink, he almost throws up, but manages to hold it in and not show weakness. Ordinarily, tequila doesn't make him sick, but so much has happened in the last few days that he is physically weak and mentally disconcerted.

---

12. Don't worry about it. Here, take a swig of tequila,"

Episode IX
Pepsi and Machete

Machete is flown on a C-130 cargo plane for the two-hour trip. From the airport he is taken to the replacement center. The center is next to the beach, on the South China Sea. Hundreds of soldiers are moving up and down the beach like aimless ants. The combat for the 196th Light Infantry Brigade of the Americal Division has been especially severe recently, so Machete is promptly assigned to his unit, given his gear, and taken to Landing Zone Hawk that same day. He has never ridden on a helicopter before, and is somewhat uneasy when the helicopter hits air turbulence and suddenly shakes. To make matters worse, the doors of the Huey helicopter have been taken off and no seat belts are provided.

Two other soldiers are in the helicopter, both with stoic faces. They are oblivious to Machete, and it seems, to the world as a whole. Finally, LZ Hawk can be seen from the helicopter. It is a hill out in the middle of mountainous jungle, in what are called free-fire zones. These are huge tracts of jungle occupied by the enemy. It is hostile country, dubbed, "Indian country" by the soldiers. Anything that moves and cannot be identified can be fired upon. Like most soldiers, Machete thinks that since he is with the "good guys," they outnumber the enemy. But this is not the case.

Machete sees that LZ Hawk is built on a steep hill, which makes it difficult to attack. Juxtaposed to battalion headquarters, on top of the hill, are artillery and mortar positions. Around the hill are fifteen bunkers made of discarded artillery shell boxes and sandbags. An infantry company is rotated every three days to man the bunkers. For the rear echelon personnel, who for some reason beyond their control find themselves on the LZ, it is a terrifying and uncomfortable experience. But for the "straight legs," as the infantry call themselves, this is a place of relative safety and comfort. Here they can bathe, eat foul-tasting hot food, and not have to walk all day long in the bush.

Inside the bunkers, which they share with rats, are crude bunk beds made of old ammo crates. Some of the soldiers sleep inside the bunkers; and others outside it because they believe if attacked, the bunker will be the first targeted. As with most beliefs, it is a matter of subjective objectivity—sometimes it works and sometimes it doesn't.

Connecting the bunkers are three-feet deep trenches from where the soldiers can take their fighting positions. Below the bunkers is strewn razor sharp wire called concertina wire. Placed in front of the wire are claymore mines and booby-trapped grenades.

The helicopter circles around the hill like a buzzard closing in on its prey. When it lands on the lower landing pad, a mortar attack begins. "Get the fuck off," yells one of the soldiers to Machete. As Machete sets his feet on the ground, the helicopter sets off. In its haste to leave, the back rotor blade tilts to the right and swiftly decapitates one of the soldiers fleeing the helicopter. Machete freezes in disbelief when the head rolls by him and it continues down the hill.

"Get your ass in here," yells someone from a foxhole. When he reaches the foxhole and jumps in, the mortar barrage ceases. He peeps his head out of the hole and surveys the damage. Parts of people are splattered on the landing pad. Several soldiers are groaning with pain as others lie in painless list.

"Fucking gook fuckers," curses the soldier, red with cornhusker contempt. "Man, I sure will be glad when I get my hands on one of those zipper head cocksuckers."

Machete takes a look at the soldier and recognizes him from the helicopter trip. His innocent, sun burnt freckles and sandy hair camouflage a spiritual brutality acquired by war.

"I'm just glad those guys killed weren't from Bravo company. You're the fucking new guy, ain't you?" he asks Machete.

"That's right," answers Machete.

"What company you in?"

"Bravo company."

"Today is your lucky day because I'm in Bravo company. We have to leave on the next chopper. Man, you really look like a fucking new guy," says Pepsi as he inspects Machete's new clothes and gear. "You've even got a new machete. What's your name?"

"They call me Machete."

"No, shit! What a fucking name."

"Who are you?"

"Pepsi."

"No shit! What a fucking name."

EPISODE X
A Dog and a Three Bear

Ese is taken to his battalion headquarters by helicopter and issued his equipment by mid-morning. By early afternoon, he is on his way to report to his unit out on a search-and-destroy mission in war zone D of the Iron Triangle. It is called the Iron Triangle because it forms a triangle on the map. It is a Viet Cong and North Vietnamese stronghold. The land is flat, with lush tropical vegetation. Unlike most soldiers, Ese does not synonymously equate war with Viet Nam. He thinks, I could dig this place if it weren't for the war.

When the helicopter is several feet from landing, one of the door gunners motions him to help jettison the supplies from the helicopter. The door gunner is markedly hasty and motions Ese to jump out after the supplies. "What, are you crazy?" he yells to the gunner, who doesn't hear him because of the noise. To his surprise, Ese is pushed out of the helicopter.

His fall is cushioned by his rucksack as he lands on his back. As the helicopter flies away, he laments, that's the last time I'll see home again. After the helicopter noise fades, he hears gunfire, and realizes that's the reason why he was thrown out. He lays there for a few moments, then notices soldiers melting out of the bush. Their clothes are badly worn and they smell terrible. Thorn and grass cuts cover their arms and faces. They seem older than they really are.

One of the soldiers approaches him and asks him in a Puerto Rican accent, "¿De dónde eres?"

"De California," he answers.

"¿Cómo te llamas?"

"Me dicen, Ese."

"Qué nombre tan raro."

"A mi me dicen Marlon porque dicen que me paresco a Marlon Brando."

"Sí, le das un parecido a él,"[1] says Ese.

Marlon tells Ese, in Spanish, "Come with me; you are in our platoon. Most of our people are out on patrol and should be here any moment now." Marlon leads him to their side of the circular perimeter. Dead logs are placed in front of every fighting position. Behind the logs are shallow holes to lay in.

Ese puts his rucksack on the ground and tells Marlon, ¿A dónde está el escusado?"

"¿El escusado? ¿Qué diablos es eso?"

"Tengo que cagar," he tells him.

"O, a unos cuantos metros para ya,"[2] says Marlon pointing to a latrine a few meters away.

Ese walks to the latrine; a one foot deep, two by four foot wide hole. He pulls his pants down and squats down to defecate. He finishes and wipes himself. As he pulls his pants up, a mortar attack begins. Mortars land around him and he doesn't know what to do, except that he should take cover. But where? A mortar falls dead center on the position to his left. It is a direct hit on a sergeant. Intestines, blood and other internal organs cover the face of his companion. The soldier wipes the blood and entrails off his face and falls catatonic.

When Ese sees that, he jumps into the latrine without hesitation. For two everlasting minutes, Ese feels like he is inside a bass drum being banged as mortar rounds land around him. He is so terrified

---

1. Where you from?" "From California," he answers."What's your name?"
   "They call me Ese" "What a rare name" "They call me Marlon because
   they say I look like Marlon Brando" "Yes, you do favor him a bit,"

2. "Where's the excuse me," "The excuse me? What in the devil is that."
   "I've got to take a shit," "Oh, a few meters that way,"

that he doesn't even smell the feces. "Help Mr. Wizard, help Mr. Wizard," he pleads. When the attack ceases, Ese jumps out of the latrine and immediately takes off his shirt. Around him are wounded and dead soldiers.

Hijola, what did I get myself into? he wonders. As the terror begins to wear off, he smells the excrement. Marlon comes over to see if he is O.K. Along with him is sergeant Three Bears, a Lakota from South Dakota. Three Bears has high cheek bones, ivory white teeth and is of medium height. This vato looks like one of those Indians that the calvary are always killing in the movies, thinks Ese.

They can't help but smirk when they see Ese. "Come over to our position; we've got some water so you can clean up, boy," says Three Bears as he thinks, this Mexican is a real character, he just got here and he's all ready into the shit. He looks like one of those bandidos that the white man is always shooting in the movies.

"You're lucky that the re-supply chopper brought water or else you wouldn't be able clean up like this. Take your pants and boots off and I'll get you some other clothes," says Three Bears.

Ese does as he is told. Three Bears pours water over him and Ese is able to get most of the muck off. Three Bears throws him a towel and says, "You still got some shit in your right ear. I'll be back in a little while." Three Bears walks away, thinking, this guy's all right. What for, I don't know? But he's all right.

Three Bears walks to where the dead soldiers are lined up. He doesn't feel much sorrow because he didn't know any of them very well; none of them were in his platoon. He has learned to befriend the least people possible. Some of the dead have been placed in green body bags that look like large, reinforced garbage bags. He looks over the dozen or so dead bodies that have yet to be covered and takes a shirt from one and the pants and boots off another. These don't seem to have much blood, and look like they should fit that new knucklehead, he calculates.

When he gets back to Ese, he tells him as he throws him the clothes, "Here, put these on."

"Where'd you get these?"

"I got them from some people who don't need them anymore," says Three Bears with his usual pragmatic reasoning. "Hurry up, because we're going on patrol to look for those mortar positions that hit us. And you and a dog are walking point."

"Me walk the point? Why is the dog walking it, too?"

"His owner just got killed and your the fucking new guy."

"Fuck it. I don't give a motherfucking fuck. Fuck the world," says Ese with senseless cockiness. "Maybe I'll get to kill somebody."

"The dog will be walking in front of you and he'll attack anything that gets in front of him. When he does, just start firing at whatever he attacks," says Three Bears. "Marlon here will be walking behind you as your backup man. Right, Marlon?"

Marlon smiles and says, "Si, patron." [3]

"I thought Marlon told me he doesn't understand English," says Ese.

"He doesn't understand things that are not to his convenience. Right, Marlon?" says Three Bears with a wink.

Marlon responds with a wide grin.

"He would be the pointman, if you hadn't come along. So now, he has you and the dog walking in front of him. He's happier than a pig in shit. No pun intended, kid. Let's move out," orders Three Bears.

Ese is thrilled and delighted that at last he is able to be out in action, fighting for the glory of his country, his family and himself. When he gets back home, everyone will know that he is a hero and good citi-

---

3. "Yes, boss."

zen, and not just an ordinary Mexican. His veteran father and uncles will be proud that he has balls.

"We're going to stick to the trails so we can get to the enemy fast without having to cut our way through. It's more dangerous this way, but we've got to do it," imparts Three Bears.

"Aquí está el perro policia, el Rin Tin Tin,"[4] announces Marlon.

The dog saw his last master die like his two previous ones. He wags his tail in hopefulness that his next master will last longer.

"O.K., dog, let's go," says Ese. He lets the dog lead.

Since Ese is left-handed, he walks down the trail with his M-16 at a forty-five degree angle downward with his left index finger on the trigger and right hand on the barrel guard, ready to pull up and fire. Ese carefully watches to the front of the German Shepherd. Stress and anticipation pump his body chemistry to the pinnacle of effectiveness. He has an intrinsic aptitude for walking point; cautious, yet foolhardy.

Along the way, Ese notices fresh feces next to the trail, which indicates that the enemy has just passed by. They walk for several kilometers before they take a break. He shares a cigarette with Marlon. "Come here, boy," he calls to the dog. The dog comes to him. Ese takes a long drag of the cigarette, holds the smoke in, grabs the dog from the muzzle and blows smoke into his nose. The dog sneezes. Marlon and Ese are amused with the dog's reaction. "Wait till we get back to the rear, dog, we're going to give you some weed and make a hippie puppy out of you."

The trail becomes more worn and used as they progress. The dog is three meters ahead of Ese where the trail turns to the right. When the dog turns right, he growls maliciously and leaps toward a Vietnamese soldier carrying an AK-47. Ese can see the soldier through the tall grass. The Vietnamese's face contorts with terror, Ese pulls his rifle up

---

4. Here is the police dog Rin Tin Tin

and shoots at the soldier. He quickly expends the bullets in his magazine. Not knowing how many enemies there are, he dives to the side of trail to reload his rifle.

Marlon didn't know what to make of the situation and has taken a position alongside the trail, as has everyone else. Marlon realizes that no one is firing at them and yells, "Ya no disparen, ya no dispare." [5]

By this time, Three Bears has come forward with the M-60 machine gunner, Cadillac and his assistant, Da-Da. "Move it up, and we'll follow you," Three Bears tells Ese.

Ese cautiously crouches around the trail and spots the dog laying on his side and panting. Behind him is Three Bears and the machine gun squad. "I guess the guy got away," says Ese.

"No thanks to you," grins Three Bears. "You guys go up the trail and guard it," he orders Cadillac and Da-Da, the platoon's best machine gun team. "Marlon, tell everybody down the line that we're taking a break and that we need a medic."

"Shit, look at this poor dog. I wonder what would have happened if he wouldn't have been in front of me?" asks Ese.

Three Bears has figured out what has happened and quizzes Ese, "Did you have your weapon on semi-automatic or full- automatic?"

"Semi."

"Mistake, Knucklehead. Always walk the point with full- automatic. Did the Vietnamese shoot?"

"I don't know."

"He didn't, because Marlon and me never heard the sound of an AK. And there aren't any spent bullet casings around. Do you know what that means?"

"No," he tells him.

"You shot the dog."

---

5. "Stop shooting, stop shooting."

While they were talking, the medic has examined the dog and tells Three Bears, "This dog's a goner; it's better if we shoot him so he won't suffer anymore."

"It's on you, Knucklehead."

"Thanks a lot, dog I owe you. I'll name my first kid after you," says Ese with remorse, before he shoots him in the head.

EPISODE XI
Contorted Silhouettes

Chuco's platoon leaves Dong Tam in the evening. They walk a few kilometers and set up for the night. In the Mekong Delta, the soldiers struggle with swamps full of: keen-edged elephant grass, prickly briers, blood-sucking leeches, snakes of all sorts, truculent mosquitoes, liver debilitating hepatitis, shit-kicking dysentery, malaria fever, knee-deep mud, dirty water, the hot sun, and mean Viet Cong.

It is very uncomfortable for everyone, but especially for Chuco, since this is his first night in a swamp. Ro-Ro notices Chuco lift his pant leg and makes a fuss when he sees a leech sucking on him. Ro-Ro goes over and uses his lit cigarette to burn it off. Instantly, the leech falls off and Chuco is relieved.

"Gracias," he tells Ro-Ro. He looks around until he finds a dry spot to sit on.

"Don't get too comfortable; we're going to set up an ambush outside the perimeter as soon as it gets dark," he tells Chuco.

The sun finally goes down like smoldering embers, dunked in a barrel of water. Ro-Ro and his squad of ten men travel quietly for several hundred yards, until they reach a well traveled rice paddy dike. This is the ambush site, and they set up with inaudible efficiency. Claymore mines, packed with plastic explosives and steel bearings which are detonated by an electrical charge provided by a battery, are placed alongside the paddy dike.

The squad is divided into five two-man teams. One of the team members sleeps, while the other stays awake. They position themselves behind some reeds a few feet from the dike. Ro-Ro is with Chuco and gives him the first two-hour watch. Ro-Ro whispers to him,

"No comienses a tirar con tu rifle, hasta que estes seguro that some-body is coming down the trail. Porque si la regas, los chinos van a saber que estamos aqui y aqui esta cabron. Una vez nos hicieron correr."

"Y porque correion?" asks Chuco.

"Porque no teniamos alas,"[1] answers Ro-Ro.

A luminous half-moon shines for the first hour of Chuco's watch. He is nervous, but glad that he is finally out in the field; the anticipation has begun to flutter away. His mind wanders and nostalgia, an age old enemy of soldiers, takes hold. He thinks of his aunts, mother and grandmother, and wishes he could be with them, sitting at the kitchen table listening to stories about the past, while his cousins, brothers and sisters argue over board or card games. If it was Saturday night, his uncles, father and grandfather would also be at another table play-ing conquián[2] and drinking beer.

He remembers his last night in Illusion when he slow danced with Sleepy Eyes. His arms were around her waist and hers around his neck. He remembers he kissed her gently on the neck and how her perfume and natural odor gave him an erection.

Abruptly, he snaps out of the mild trance and notices rushing clouds overhead. The clouds obscure the moonlight and form contort-ed silhouettes on the ground. It seems to Chuco that some of these are actually Viet Cong moving in on them. His body becomes rigid, his face tightens with fear and he pulls the trigger, but the rifle doesn't fire.

At this moment Ro-Ro rouses and whispers, "¿Que pasa, calabaza?"[3]

"Nada, nada," says Chuco with great relief, realizing it was only the shadows.

---

1. "Don't start shooting until you are sure that somebody is coming down the trail. Because if you blow it, the Chinese are going to know we're here. And it's a motherfucker here. One time they made us run."
   "Why did you run?"
   "Because we didn't have wings,"
2. a card game
3. "What's happening dummy?"

EPISODE XII
A Wretched Night

In the Northern Central Highlands, temperatures are extreme. During the day, the high temperature reaches 110 degrees, and at night, falls to 40 degrees. The mountains are steep and high. Constant technological clobbering by high explosive artillery, jet fighter attacks, two thousand pound bombs dropped by B-52 bombers, scorching napalm, and Agent Orange defoliant have taken their toll on the land. Since most animals kill exclusively for food, they have left for safer and more rational ground. Only humans remain.

Machete's calves have become hard, like his head, from walking up and down mountains for the last month. It is midday. The sun and heat are intense. They have run out of water and are looking for more. From the top of a mountain, they can see a small valley with abandoned rice paddies. Machete is the pointman and leads his platoon of thirty-five men down the mountain.

When they reach the valley, all they find is stagnant rice paddy water. "We've got to move on until we can find some moving water to drink," orders Pepsi, who is the acting platoon sergeant. A week before Machete joined the platoon, half of the platoon had either been killed or wounded in an ambush. This made Pepsi, the non-commissioned officer in charge. The LT, as everyone calls him, is technically the officer in charge; but because of his inexperience, Pepsi gives most of the orders. But he gives them as if they are suggestions to the LT, so as not to disrupt the hierarchy in the chain of command.

The men become more desperate for water as they walk the edge of the tree line next to the paddies. The water is dark brown and smells terrible. Their mouths are cotton-dry and lips are cracked. The men are to the point of breaking rank and drinking the water. Finally, they reach a spot where the water moves in tiny trickles from one rice paddy to another. "All right, only five guys at a time can fill a canteen of water at a time," orders Pepsi. Since they work in such small units, trying to out-guerilla the guerillas, they are always leery of ambush.

Machete is one of the first five to get to the water. "Remember to use your iodine tablets," warns Pepsi. He is a typical infantry sergeant out in the bush: a draftee, twenty years old, from a working-class family, and wants to keep himself and the men alive, so they can go home in one piece.

"Hijo de su pinche madre, como tengo sed,"[1] says Machete to himself as he brushes away the insects on the top of the slow moving trickle. Most of the men are so thirsty that they don't heed Pepsi's warning, and drink the water without iodine tablets.

Before all the men can get water, Cobra helicopters that resemble flying sharks, swoop in on them firing mini-guns and rockets. Some men are killed or wounded before they can find cover in the tree line. Pepsi begins to fire at the helicopters. "Don't fire at the helicopters," orders the LT.

"I don't give a good-flying-fuck, sir; they're trying to kill us," answers Pepsi.

"Get on the horn, LT, and tell battalion to call them off," yells Pepsi.

The lieutenant gets on the radio and frantically says, "Delta-Two-Five, this is Charlie-Rover-Two. We are being attacked by our own choppers, repeat, being attacked by our own choppers. Call them off. Call them off, over."

"Roger that Charlie-Rover-Two, but you are not supposed to be in that position over," answers Delta-Two-Five.

"Listen, Delta-Two-Five, if those cobras come at us again, we're

---

1. "Son-of-a-bitch, I'm thirstier than shit,"

going to shoot them down," threatens Pepsi on the radio. "Call in two medevacs; we've got some dead and wounded. Besides, we have called in our correct position. You're the ones who fucked up, over!"

The blood of the casualties has turned the water in the rice paddy like red kool-aid. Some of the dead bodies occasionally twitch from muscle spasms. Most of the dead and wounded are new guys, except for Bones, the medic, who has been with Pepsi since they both arrived in Viet Nam. "Relax, Bones," he comforts, as he tries to stop the blood exuding from three bullet wounds. "The medevacs are coming to pick you up. Everything is going to be O.K. and you'll be back in Cass City before you know it." Bones doesn't say anything as he emits a soft sigh and closes his eyes.

"Fucking stupid, stupid fuckers; they killed Bones," says Pepsi, as he cries and holds Bones' head on his lap. "Stupid, stupid fuckers. Come on fuckers! Come at us again and we'll shoot your fucking asses down!" says Pepsi, looking toward the sky.

In a matter of minutes, two helicopters arrive and load the wounded first, then the dead. "Stupid fuckers; they killed Bones," mumbles Pepsi as the helicopters fly off.

Pepsi gathers himself and orders, "Saddle up, we've got some more humping to do." He goes to Machete and tells him, "We've got to get out of here fast 'cause the enemy knows exactly where we're at now, thanks to those idiot hot-shot pilots. We gotta didi it out of here now. We're going to backtrack because the gooks won't expect that. We're going to night-lodger at that gook cemetery we passed along the way, so let's get moving."

Machete stares at the setting sun and it reminds him of the red and orange snow cones he would buy at Kiko's store. He wishes he had one now. The rag-tag platoon reaches a tiny cemetery atop a small hill. The cemetery is one that was used by the local villagers before they were forced to re-locate. Pepsi makes sure all the soldiers are assigned their positions around the hill and that they dig foxholes. Then he and Machete dig their foxhole for a couple of feet until they hit some wood. "What the hell is this?" asks Machete.

"I don't know, but I think I've got a good idea," answers Pepsi as he clears more dirt away. "Just like I thought. It's a fucking wood coffin. Man, these sure are some lazy people. They didn't even bury this gook six foot under."

"Fuck it. I ain't doing no more digging. I'll just sleep on top of this dead gook," concedes Machete.

"Me too," says Pepsi. "You can take the first guard."

"Thanks for nothing, Pepsi."

The night is dark and visibility is zero. Machete begins to feel a pain in his abdomen and listens to his intestines growl. To his left, he hears what sounds like a snorting buck. Naw, that can't be. There aren't any deer over here, he guesses. His pain becomes worse. Abruptly, he jumps out of the foxhole, pulls down his pants and like an erupting volcano, streams of fiery razor-lava pour out of his anus. Occasionally, he makes a relieving, snorting buck sound.

That's what that noise was, he reflects. Some of the guys have the shits. I bet it was from not putting the iodine tablets in the water.

Pepsi stirs and asks, "What's all that farting shit going on?"

"A lot of the guys have the shits, Pepsi. And it hurts like hell."

"Good," he says. "Don't say you weren't warned. Now I don't have to pull guard 'cause you guys will be up all night shitting. Even the North Vietnamese won't get close to your skunk asses."

This is Machete's most wretched night of his young life.

EPISODE XIII
Shampion in My Country

Two months of living in the jungle are taking their toll on Ese's platoon. For two months, they have not changed their clothes, brushed their teeth or bathed. Once in a while, they can play cards for thirty minutes or so, but even then, noise discipline must be maintained, and they can only speak in whispers. The stress of the constant contact with the enemy is pushing many of the soldiers to their physical and emotional limits.

One of the soldiers, Deputy Dawg, is no longer coherent. Everyone leaves him alone and lets him walk drag; the last man to walk in the file. He keeps to himself and mumbles his existence away.

"Three Bears, we've got to do something about Deputy Dawg. He's really out of it," says Ese.

"I tried to about a month ago. I went and told Captain America about it."

"What did he say?"

"He said that he was just faking it, to try to get out of the field."

"Naw, I don't think so. This guy is really out of it. Look at him," says Ese, as he turns his head to the right where Deputy Dawg is sitting, with his legs crossed and mumbling.

"Yeah, I know. A couple of Sundays ago, when the Padre came and gave Mass, I told him about Deputy."

"And what did he say?"

"That it is the Lord's will that Deputy fight against the Godless communists."

"Fight! As you would say: 'He's about as worthless as tits on a boar hog.' All he is going to do is get himself killed. Or worse yet, get one

71

of us killed."

"No shit, Knucklehead. And even when he was right, he couldn't even shoot straight; he couldn't hit a bull in the ass with a handful of mustard seeds. He started getting this way ever since his fiancée wrote him a Dear John letter. Cadillac read it and he said she simply wrote, 'Dear Deputy: Yours is bigger but his is here.'"

"Three Bears, it's the lieutenant on the horn and he wants to talk to you," interrupts Yo-Yo the radioman.

Three Bears picks up the receiver and his face becomes radiant with joy. "Roger that," he says as he signs off. "Give the word down the line to get ready to move out. Man, we're going to be shitting in tall cotton this evening."

"What, what the hell's going on?" asks Ese.

"We've got to find a landing zone and clear it for the helicopters to pick up our platoon and take us to a bridge that's next to a vill. We'll be guarding the bridge at night because they expect an attack soon."

"You mean we won't have to hump the bush?"

"That's right, Knucklehead, you're so smart."

The platoon finds a landing zone quickly and are airlifted to a bridge next to a well-populated town. When close to the town, Ese can see from the air that the main street is unpaved and about a mile long. Dwellings of various sizes and materials are closely clustered throughout the small city. People on foot, motorcycles, jeeps and army trucks scamper like tiny insects. He can see that the bridge, at one end of the town, crosses a serpentine river.

They are dropped off on the grounds of a demolished Buddhist temple. The dust created by the helicopters and intense heat makes Ese feel as if he is in one those desolate towns in spaghetti westerns.

Three Bears confers with the lieutenant, and they decide that Three Bears will take half of the men to one end of the bridge and the lieutenant will take the other half to the opposite end.

Several meters away from the bridge, Ese and Three Bears sense the Vietnamese are uneasy with their presence. Marlon and Cadillac attract some kids by giving them candy. When they reach the bridge, Cadillac breaks out in a hand-clapping dance and says to Da-Da, "Yo man, we're going to be living the life of fat rats. No humping for three days. And we might even gets some poontang. Ain't that right, home-boy?"

"You…you just ain' ta…ta talking shit," answers Da-Da who stutters when he is excited.

"Shit, we might even get some pussy for the lieutenant," says Ese.

"That pooty-booty ain't had pussy since pussy had him. Fuck him in his neck," says Cadillac. "Ain't that right, home-boy," he tells Da-Da as he gives him a black power handshake.

The men settle under the shade of the bridge. During the day, the bridge is open and maintained by a South Vietnamese Army unit, cantoned next to the bridge. At night, Ese's platoon will stand guard.

For the first time since he has been in Viet Nam, Ese has contact with Vietnamese civilians. Hundreds of people cross the bridge from dawn to dusk. Some of the people bring fried fish, noodles or potatoes to sell, which the soldiers gobble up as soon as they buy them.

Night is gradually defeating day. Sitting on top of the bridge, Ese and Cadillac observe two young girls beckoning them from a hut across the road. The rest of the men are lounging under the bridge, so Ese and Cadillac think it's a good time to slink across the road and see what the girls want.

Like two alley cats armed with M-16's, they prudently strut their way across the road. They reach the girls, who look like sisters. One is slightly prettier than the other.

The girls scrutinize Ese and Cadillac and begin to argue. Ese and

Cadillac don't understand what they are saying, but when one curls her fingers around Ese's straight black hair and says, "Number one." Then she touches Cadillac's hair and says, "Number ten." It becomes obvious to them that they are arguing about race.

Ese and Cadillac are startled when a Honda 50 motorcycle comes to a noisy halt behind them. They turn like whirlwinds and point their rifles at a cantankerous old man's head. He is dauntless to the rifles as he gets off the motorcycle, ranting and raving with a switch in hand. He upbraids the girls as he hits them with the switch and forces them on his motorcycle. He drives away rancorously.

"That must've been their grandpappy," says Cadillac in his Georgia accent.

"No shit," says Ese with extreme disappointment. "It looks like I'm going to have to whack-off. But at least we got a bottle of whiskey."

The two return to the bridge which has now been closed off. Soon the GIs will take over guarding the bridge. "I'll go down and get the bottle of whiskey," Ese tells Cadillac, as he goes under the bridge.

Marlon, Three Bears, Da-Da and Yo-Yo are playing spades. For the first time in two months, they are able to play without having to worry about noise discipline and are somewhat relaxed. Ese grabs the bottle from his rucksack and offers some to the guys. They all refuse because they are drinking beer and smoking marijuana.

"Remember, we've got a volleyball game with the gook soldiers in the morning, Knucklehead. We're playing them for cokes," Three Bears reminds Ese.

"Right. Me and Cadillac will take the first guard; we'll wake you up when it's your turn."

As Ese walks up toward the bridge, he hears the familiar arguing.

"Quit sandbagging, Marlon," complains Three Bears.

"Me no sandbag, Tres Osos. I shampion in my country."

"Hell Marlon, Puerto Rico ain't no country," says Yo-Yo.

"Yes, it my country."

"You didn't even speak a word of English when you got here. How did you get in this army anyway?" asks Yo-Yo.

"I drafted from my country."

As they gradually get drunk, Ese and Cadillac talk of home and how they had it made. They talk of how things are going to be even better once they return. "I've got forty-nine days and a wake-up left in country. I'm going to be one happy motherfucka when I gets on that freedom bird back to the world. I'm going to be bookin' across the pond like a big dog, bigger than shit, bigger than do-do," says Cadillac with glee. "The first thing I'm going to do when I get back to the world is get me some whiskey and cock at the Sophisticated Soul in Augusta, GA. Brown Sugar works there and she told me she'd be waiting for me. That's one fine-looking mama. You ought to see her when she puts on a tight black mini-skirt and wears some of them red come-fuck-me high heel shoes. Boy, I wish you could see how fine that hammer is."

"What are you going to do if Jody Cock-Blocker is there?"

"Shit, as soon as Brown Sugar sees me, she'll drop that nigger in a flash."

"Are you going to eat that pussy?"

"Boy, you're sick. You sounds just like a white boy. Bloods don't do that shit. That's nasty. If I can't buy it at the grocery store, I don't eat it," says Cadillac with disgust.

At one point, Ese asks Cadillac about a soldier they called Panther Man, who was killed before Ese joined the platoon. "Yo man, that was one righteous brother from Chi-town," he says with enthusiasm. "He used to be in the Black Panthers until he got into a hassle with the pigs, and the judge gave him a choice of going to prison or the army.

That man didn't take no shit from nobody. You would have liked him cause homeboy could sure shuck and jive."

"The last time I saw him was on standdown, and he was hanging out with some militant bloods who were AWOL. From there, he went AWOL too. A couple of weeks later, we found out that the MPs went looking for him in the vill where he was shacking with some Vietnamese 'hos. He had a shoot out with the military pigs. He kilt two and wounded three. But they got him, too. Shot him twenty times and kilt him, I hear," says Cadillac with remorse. "That blood had a lot of heart."

Ese and Cadillac stay up half the night drinking whiskey. After they finish the bottle, they drink beer. When they are sufficiently inebriated, they wake Three Bears to take the guard. They walk underneath the bridge where all the soldiers are sleeping in hammocks. "Get your big candy-ass up, puto," says Ese.

"Fuck, you smell like a burnt taco soaked in whiskey," says Three Bears rubbing his eyes.

"Tacos! I could use one. I sure do miss tacos," laughs Ese as he nestles into a hammock and falls asleep.

"Wake up God-dammit. We have a volleyball game to play," orders Three Bears.

"Oh shit, I feel like fuck," says Ese with his mouth cotton-dry and a headache that makes him feel like an unabridged cadaver.

"Let's go, Knucklehead."

"I need a beer."

"I thought you would. Here," says Three Bears handing him one.

Ese winces as he takes the first drink. He guzzles the rest on the second drink. "Oh man, I think I'm going to throw up." He runs to the rivers edge and vomits.

"That's some nasty shit you're puking there, buddy," says Three Bears. "It looks like you're having an abortion through your mouth."

"Man, I need another beer," says Ese as he washes his face with river water.

Three Bears hands him another and says, "Let's go."

The rest of the platoon joins them, and with M-16s and machine guns, they walk to the net together. The Vietnamese soldiers are about the size of Ese or smaller. Since most the GIs are bigger, they feel that they should be able to win with little effort. But they don't realize that the Vietnamese play regularly.

They play the best two of three games. Ese does not play and sits on the sidelines next to Deputy Dawg, drinking beer and heckling Three Bears. Marlon is allowed to play the second half of the first game. Every time the ball is hit towards Marlon, he closes his eyes and either misses it or hits it out-of-bounds.

Some of the more competitive GIs become upset. "Get him out of here," they demand.

"I shampion in my country. I shampion," says Marlon.

"Get your fucking ass out of here, Marlon," the GIs tell him.

"Chuleta, coño, como son serios estos tipos," Marlon tells Ese.

"No te apures. Tomate una cerveza,"[1] advises Ese. Ese understands that Marlon cannot take the game seriously.

The GIs win the first game by two points. Towards the end of the second game, Marlon is demanding that they let him play. "I shampion. I shampion," he keeps saying.

"Let him play, let him play," shouts and panders Ese on the sidelines.

Out of camaraderie, Marlon is permitted to play. Again, he closes his eyes when the ball comes towards him, and either misses it or hits it out of bounds allowing the Vietnamese to win.

---

1. "Darn, these guys sure are serious,"
   "Don't worry. Drink another beer,"

"God damn you, Marlon, you lost the game for us," complain the soldiers.

"I shampion. I shampion," says Marlon, winking his eye toward Ese.

The third game is intense and well-played. Again Marlon and Ese start a ruckus on the sidelines for Marlon to play. "Hey, you puto Tres Osos, I haven't played. Marlon can play for me. He's in our squad," demands Ese.

"That's right," yells Deputy Dawg, awakening from his existential detour. "That's right, he can play for me too," he finishes before he lapses.

Three Bears and his squad get the message, and allow Marlon to play as the loquacious Marlon continues to clamor, "I shampion in my country. I shampion." The GIs eventually lose the third game.

Episode XIV
¿Quien Es? La Virgen Es

Every other day for three months, Chuco has been walking the point. Today, he is told to be extra careful because there have been reports of increased Viet Cong activity in the area. At first, Chuco didn't know the difference between the Viet Cong and the North Vietnamese army, or the NVA, as they are referred to by the GIs. One day, he asked Ro-Ro what the difference was, and was told, "Guacha carnal,[1] the Viet Congs are from the South and they don't wear army uniforms. They can be the farmers we see during the day, pero en la noche[2] when it gets dark, they can turn into VC. The North Vietnamese are from North Viet Nam. They are regular soldiers, and not guerillas like the Viet Cong. Pero cuidate, por que[3] they can all kill you."

About noon, Chuco leads the Platoon out of a marsh into a lightly wooded area. The platoon takes a break and all the men light up cigarettes. Nicotine is the most important drug for infantry soldiers and the one most readily supplied by the military. Ro-Ro comes up to Chuco and tells him, "Guacha carnal, the lieutenant wants your squad to go look for a night-lodger for the whole company because we are going to re-group with them tonight." Ro-Ro brings out a map and shows him the approximate location that they think will be a good location. "Ponte extra trucha por que estos swamps are full of chinos,"[4] cautions Ro-Ro.

Chuco sets out with his squad of six men. Walking directly behind him, is Feo, followed by Cafe, Impala, Shotgun and Quelite the medic.

---

1. "Look brother,
2. but at night
3. but be careful because
4. "Be extra careful these swamps are full of Chinese,"

The trail winds in and out of marshes into wooded areas as they follow a stream. Chuco knows better than to follow a stream, because it is inviting an ambush; but they are so tired, he takes the easy way.

Progressively the grass and foliage become thicker, and Chuco takes out his machete and clears a path. On one of the swings of the machete, his chain, with medallions of the Virgen de Guadalupe and Jesus Christ around his neck, snaps. Somehow, he feels the chain break and frantically looks for the medallions on the ground. His heart begins to throb against his rib cage and the blood in his veins feels like cold needles. For a few agonizing moments, Chuco frantically searches and feels the grass strewn ground for the medallions. Miraculously, he finds them and a blush of relief fills his chest.

When they come to the foot of a hill, they are astounded by a fairy tale scene of tall trees and rocks covered with dark green moss. The stream is now cool and so is the air. They are totally immersed with the pleasant environment and forget about noise discipline. "Mira que toda madre.[5] It reminds me of Pine Park back home," says Feo as he caresses the moss.

"A mi tambien.[6] It's just like Mooney Groove back home," says Shotgun.

Chuco soon catches himself and says, "O.K. be quiet...that's enough; we've got to be quiet. Vamonos de aquí pronto,"[7] he says with urgency.

As he leads them across the stream, the clacking sounds of an AK-47 resonate. "I'm hit," yells Feo, just behind him. Chuco helps him to his side of the stream. A bullet has hit Feo in the leg. His face becomes red with pain.

Feo cannot move and has no choice but to lay on the trail. Chuco

5. "Look, everything is so pretty.
6. "For me too.
7. Let's get out of here now,"

thinks, Me descuento y dejo este vato aquí.[8] Naw, I can't do that. Y de todos modos, para donde corro.[9] Chuco is terrified when he hears the Vietnamese calling out to them, but can't see them because of the giant elephant grass, "Chinguen sus madres [10] you motherfuckers," he shouts to the Vietnamese as he fires his M-16 towards the sound of their voices.

I got to do like those Chicano soldiers told us at the airport in San Francisco. Keep my ass down and keep firing back, he remembers. As the squad leader, he realizes he has made a great error by not carrying more ammunition. He figured it was just a routine patrol. Como soy pendejo,[11] there is no such thing as a routine patrol, he scolds himself. The dreadful calculation of what the Vietnamese will do to them if they are caught convinces him that they must fight to the end. His pride and machismo also add to his decision to stay. Besides, he reckons that it is more dangerous to run than to stay put.

He shouts across the stream "Ese Quelite, ¿a quien le dieron?"

"Al pinche Impala le pagaron las luces y he can't see. Y el Café está muerto. Y a mi me chingaron una mano un escante."

"¿En aqual te dieron?"

"En la mano izquierda." [12]

"Consider yourself lucky; at least it ain't your manuela hand." [13]

"Hijo de su, como me duele," [14] says Feo, holding his leg in agony. "How come in the cowboy movies it doesn't seem to hurt when they

---

8. Should I split and leave this guy here.

9. And anyway where can I run too.

10. "Fuck your mamas

11. I sure am stupid,

12. "Hey Quelite, who'd they hit."
   "Impala got his lights knocked out and he can't see. Café is dead
   And they messed up my hand a bit."
   "Which one got hit."
   "My left hand."

13. jack-off hand."

14. "Son-of-a-bitch it hurts,"

get wounded, like it does me," he says panting and breathing hard.

"Quelite, how's the radio?"

"Esta chingado."

"No te apures. De cincho Ro-Ro y el sonso de la Liebre con sus ore-jotas oieron los balasos. Y ya no tardan de llegar." [15]

Quelite and the squad are in a gulch, the one with the green moss. But now it feels more like a haunted gulch than a fairy tale.

"You vatos cover us from behind and I'll cover us from the front," says Chuco, as he lays down and points his rifle to his front. The trail turns to the right three meters ahead. The only cover he finds is an old tree stump that doesn't provide for more than a few inches of cover. He makes sure Feo gets equal protection from the stump.

Each second seems like a minute. Without warning, a young North Vietnamese soldier, about the same age as Chuco, jumps from a rock where the trail curves and faces Chuco. He is wearing a dark green North Vietnamese uniform, with a red handkerchief tied around his neck. His AK-47 is at port arms. They look at each other eye to eye for a moment. Since Chuco is lying down and has his weapon pointed and ready to fire in that direction, he has the advantage. He fires his weapon on automatic, and unloads fourteen bullets into his enemy's chest. The Vietnamese falls back, but Chuco cannot see where he fell because of the grass. He is running out of bullets and he fears that more Vietnamese maybe behind the one he shot.

No more enemy soldiers appear. Chuco tells Feo as he prepares to throw a grenade, "Cuidate, voy a tirar una granada." [16] He throws the grenade where he thinks the soldier is at. When it goes off, Feo winces in pain as he grabs his right thigh. "Hijo de la chingada me chingates

---

15. "It's fucked up."
   "Don't worry. It's a cinch Ro-Ro and that big eared Liebre heard
   the shooting. They should be here soon."
16. "Watch yourself, I'm going to throw a grenade."

la otra pierna con tu grananda, baboso." [17]

"Sorry about that, carnal, I couldn't help it. But you should have kept down." After what seems like an eternity, Chuco hears some movement, but can't see through the thick elephant grass. "¿Quién es?" he shouts.

"La virgen es, pendejo," [18] answers Ro-Ro sarcastically.

"Man, I sure am glad you vatos are here," says Chuco with great relief, when the guys reach him. Liebre finds the Vietnamese soldier still alive. With one of his legs blown off and dragging his intestines, he makes a final effort to bury his weapon by feebly throwing pinches of dirt on the rifle. Liebre walks up to him and shoots him in the head. Hijo, these sure are some hard bastards to kill," he says with respect intermingled with disdain.

"It's the captain on the radio" says Patillas, a perpetually smiling soldier with long sideburns, handing the handset to Ro-Ro.

"That's right, sir. We have one KIA, two badly wounded and one slightly wounded. We need a helicopter to dust these men off, over."

"We have called in for a helicopter, but there is only room for the two badly wounded. The dead soldier and the other one will have to wait until tomorrow morning because I have some soldiers from my platoon that need to go on R&R, over."

"But sir, the man needs medical attention, over," petitions Ro-Ro.

"You heard what I said, sergeant. Carry the dead soldier to our rendezvous point for tomorrow and then we'll dust him and the wounded one off, over," concludes the captain.

"Roger that sir, over and out. That fucking captain has his kiss-asses going on R&R and forgets about our dead camarada. Me la juro que le voy a dar en la madre a ese hijo de chucha," [19] says Ro-Ro, with his face

---

17 "You stupid shit, you fucked up my other leg with your grenade."

18. "Who is it?"

"It's the virgin stupid,"

in a twisted rage of anger.

The dust-off helicopter arrives and Feo and Impala are put on it.

"Let's move out," orders Ro-Ro.

Chuco continues walking the point. He walks for a few kilometers, when he feels a slight pressure below his knees and a popping sound. Immediately, he realizes he has set off a booby-trapped wire. Before he can say anything, a blast goes off behind him. Dirt, rocks and pieces of wood hit his back, before he falls to the ground unconscious.

---

19. I swear I'm going to fuck up that son-of-a-bitch."

EPISODE XV
Defeat

For four months, Machete and his company have been humping the bush. Only once, since he has been in country, has his company been back to their firebase. Time drags by slowly, like that of a prisoner in solitary confinement, or a month for a five year old child. In two days, they are scheduled to go on standdown and rest for three days and two nights by a beach of the South China Sea. For two nights, they will not pull guard, eat C-rations, go without water or walk the mountains like mountain sheep. And more importantly, they will not be under constant attack or fear of attack.

Machete walked point for a couple of months, but has now switched over to the M-60 machine gun the main fire power of light infantry units. The point and carrying the machine gun, are two of the most dangerous positions in the bush. Machete prefers to carry the machine gun because it has the most fire power, which gives him a sense of immense authority and importance. He knows he can do the most damage to the enemy, and they will concentrate on trying to kill him. This gives him a feeling of being chingon—a bad motherfucker.

After seeing his comrades wounded or killed, he has come to develop a growing hatred for Vietnamese, not just the Viet Cong or North Vietnamese, but all Vietnamese.

Everything goes well that day and night, no enemy contact. In the morning, they are ordered to head west and set up a perimeter around a clump of trees in the middle of a rice paddy. They are told that a company of North Vietnamese is camped here. Artillery is called in and the earth convulses savagely. Debris and parts of trees are blown in all directions. For fifteen minutes, the barrage is relentless.

"Let's move it," orders Pepsi, "our platoon is going in first." The soldiers move in cautiously, expecting to encounter resistance. But to their surprise, they meet none. Instead, they find dead North Vietnamese soldiers scattered everywhere. Some whole and others in bits and pieces. The dead remind Machete of the sugar beet plants he used to kill. The soldiers are happy, like kids in a playground, as they take souvenirs from the deceased. Pepsi, in particular, is fond of cutting off the ears of Vietnamese soldiers and making a necklace of them to hang around his neck.

Once in a while, Machete will complain when some of the ears begin to smell foul and tells him, "Take that shit off, it smells bad." Machete has begun to enjoy torturing the enemy and has become better at keeping a victim alive for longer periods of time.

"Fuck, we sure caught the gooks off-guard this time. Look at these dead gooks; there must be at least a hundred of them."

"Yeah, we got them good," says Dago Red, Machete's assistant gunner, with satisfaction.

Pepsi approaches Machete and Dago Red and tells them, "Let's get a move on; we've got to prepare a landing zone for the whole company to be choppered out. The jarheads have gotten ambushed bad and we need to go help them." With remarkable efficiency, the soldiers are delivered to their destination, one hundred miles away.

Machete's squad is the point squad and he volunteers to lead with his M-60 machine gun. He walks up to a well-used winding mountain trail. Fuck, this is a freeway. It's probably a main artery of the Ho Chi Minh trail, surmises Machete. He walks up a hill, turns a curve, and he can't believe that he has caught three North Vietnamese soldiers walking lackadaisically, unaware that he is in front of them. I thought so, he thinks as he braces the machine gun with his arms to his hip and fires. Look at those two guys on the right, they're holding hands like queers.

He squeezes the trigger and mows down the half-stepping soldiers. They fall like silhouettes in a shooting gallery. An exalted vehemence aerates his ego. I fucked them up good, me los chingue. Three less communist gook motherfuckers in this world. I'm glad I sent these godless bastards to hell, he concludes.

Machete and Dago Red make sure the Vietnamese are dead, then place the M-60 in front of the trail for defense. Pepsi and Teacher first inspect, then pillage the bodies of their belongings. They find the usual fare of sentimental momentos found on dead soldiers: letters, little flags, pictures of family and girlfriends in wallets, with a few bills of small denominations. Machete only asks for some of the money. "What the fuck do I want with gook pictures or flags," he says bitingly.

As Machete proceeds to walk point, Pepsi booby-traps the bodies by placing grenades under them that will explode when the body is moved. "We and the gooks are doing the same thing to each other, like those cartoon characters in Mad Magazine's Spy vs. Spy. That damn Chingo is one crazy fucker. He just can't kill enough gooks," he tells Dago Red.

"I know," he agrees. "We all hate them, but not like Chingo," says Dago Red, referring to Machete as Chingo, as he is now known in the platoon.

"Maybe it's because he kind of looks like one."

"Holy shit, don't your ever let him hear you say that or he'll go bananas on you," warns Dago Red.

The jungle trail becomes increasingly narrower, as smaller trails flow into it like rivers to an ocean. Machete is told to take a narrow trail heading east. He walks a couple of kilometers before he finds the first dead Marine. The dead Marine's face is expressionless. Flies and ants swarm over his face and in and out of his mouth and nose. Better him than me, is the only thing Machete can think of.

As Machete's company warily walks into the area, they find only three live Marines. The rest of the hundred or odd soldiers are dead. "What happened to you guys," asks Pepsi as Coco the medic injects morphine into the wounded soldier.

"There's zipper-heads all over this place," he says painfully. They had us surrounded," he is able to say, before he tumbles into celestial joy from the morphine.

"Coño, we'd better get this guy out of here or he's going to die," says Coco in his New York Puerto Rican accent."

Pepsi is informed on the radio that helicopters are coming to evacuate the dead and wounded. Some soldiers set up their standard circular perimeter, while others police bodies for evacuation. A small clearing has been prepared for the first helicopters that swoop in like birds diving for fish in a lake. The first three helicopters go in and out unmolested and are able to evacuate the wounded and some dead. The fourth helicopter is not as fortunate and two mortars blow it up. Machete can see from a short distance that a door gunner is trapped inside the helicopter and is burned alive. He can see that he is screaming in agony, but he can't hear him because of all the noise. What a fucked up way to go, he laments.

Mortars and small arms fire come from all directions toward the GIs. Machete's platoon is dug in on the side of the perimeter that is taking the most fire. Bullets and shrapnel perforate the entire perimeter. Bullets buzz by like agitated killer bees. Artillery and jets are not called in because the Vietnamese are dug in too close to the GIs.

The fighting becomes more intense. The Vietnamese attempt to overrun the GIs. North Vietnamese hard-core and crack infantry skillfully move from bushes and trees advancing on the GIs. The GIs fire back in rotating sporadic bursts, in order to conserve ammunition, maintain a steady line of fire, and to keep the barrels of their weapons from overheating and then warping after they cool off. They, too, are hard-core and crack warriors when it comes to fighting to stay alive.

"Come on, hijos de sus chingadas madres. Come and get it, putos," yells Machete. The situation is rapidly deteriorating for the GIs. The Vietnamese are steadily advancing. Machete goes wild, gets up from his position and charges the enemy. Bullets whiz by him and don't harm him, as if he is wearing an Indian ghost coat.

Machete's head swirls with mad colors of ferocity. He remembers the stories his father would tell him about the battles he fought under Pancho Villa, in the Mexican Revolution.

He slays several of the enemy and forces the rest to retreat. He has also inspired his fellow soldiers to advance. It is Machete's initiative, for the most part, that has kept the enemy from overrunning their perimeter. The GIs move back to their defensive positions because they don't have the fire power to hold a complete offensive position.

There are many wounded and some dead. The lieutenant has been killed. The captain is wounded and can no longer command. Pepsi is now in charge of the platoon. The twenty-year-old buck sergeant is a sagacious leader and astute tactician. He orders all the food, water and ammunition to be gathered from the dead and evenly distributed. He makes sure the remaining fire power is uniformly spread around his section of the perimeter.

Machete and Dago Red's position is next to Pepsi and Duck, the radioman. All night long, the enemy tries to overtake the GIs. Machete's position in particular is targeted and focused on by the Vietnamese. The GIs hold on with tenacity. No one gets any sleep. Sleep deprivation is something the GIs have adjusted to. But unbeknownst to them, their physiology and circadian rhythms have been radically and permanently altered.

Morning brings on a horrendous sight of dead. Torpid bodies lay everywhere. The smell of gunpowder coupled with dead human meat gives off a sinister barbecue aroma. Violent and intense sunrays escalate the decomposition. Marinated in blood, the defunct commence to bloat and turn purple-black. A putrid effluvium engulfs the jungle. The air is saturated with filth. On the second day, the bodies burst like over-ripe honeydew melons replete with maggots. Little white worms emerge, wriggling and struggling to survive off dead matter. A law of nature: All living things must eat something which was once alive.

The attrition is taking a heavy toll on the soldiers. Over fifty percent of the company has either been killed or wounded. No one has gotten any sleep. Water, food and ammunition are running low. On the third day, the U.S. Air Force drops resupplies from airplanes. It falls outside the perimeter, and resupplies the enemy instead.

"Are we ever going to get out of here?" Machete asks Pepsi.

"Hellfire! Shit, yeah!" confirms Pepsi.

"I hope your right. Man, I sure do hate these gooks." Machete tells Pepsi. "I can't wait until I can get my hands on one of those gook-communist-motherfuckers. And to think I didn't want to come and fight these motherfuckers. These cocksuckers are trying to take over the world. I'd rather fight them over here than back home. Sure, there are some messed up things that we Mexicans have to deal with, but the good old U.S. of A. is still the freest country in the world. And you can be whatever you want to be."

"Shut up, Chingo, cause here they come again," says Pepsi.

The Vietnamese are more determined than ever to eliminate the besieged GIs. Bullets fly around the perimeter like flies over a carcass. The enemy now concentrate their attack to the left of Machete's platoon. Several GIs are wounded and cannot move from their positions. Like sharks smelling the blood of their wounded prey, the Vietnamese assault with an extreme vehemence.

Machete and Pepsi cannot come to their aid because it is all they can do to keep the enemy off themselves. Like a character out of a comic book, Coco, the medic rushes to aid four wounded soldiers. He reaches them, grabs one of the wounded and carries him to safety. He comes back for a second soldier, and as he is running with him on his shoulder, a bullet hits his right leg. He grimaces with pain, but he is able to carry the wounded soldier to safety.

As the medic hobbles back to the two remaining soldiers, another bullet hits him in the shoulder. He is able to withstand the pain and rescue another soldier, but not without getting shot in his left leg again. The medic's determination and pride give him the fortitude he needs to go back for the last GI. As he is carrying him to safety, a bullet hits him in the back, but he continues nonetheless. When he reaches safety, he unloads the soldier and falls dead.

Pepsi moves to the position that was left vacant by the soldiers that were rescued by the medic. Several Vietnamese rush Machete's position and he is able to kill a few of them just several feet from him. Machete hears a click to his side. He looks up and it is an enemy soldier pointing his jammed AK-47 at him. Machete shoots him dead. He grabs the dead body and places it in front of him as a substitute for a sandbag.

The situation becomes progressively worse. After six days, the food and water completely run out, and the GIs begin to eat weeds. "I don't know what's worse: The flies, the thirst, the hunger, or the stinking dead bodies," says Machete to Pepsi, who have now consolidated their position. He turns around behind himself and sees a soldier with an open arm wound. "Man! look at that meat on that arm. It looks good huh, Pepsi?" Pepsi turns around, doesn't say anything, but gives a depraved grin.

Most of the dead no longer look like human remains. They seem like rancid lumps of meat used by flies and ants as a smorgasbord. Of the one hundred and nineteen men in Machete's company, there are thirty-two wounded, twenty-three not wounded and the rest are dead.

On the seventh day, the battalion commander and the sergeant major, flying in a helicopter, have figured out the situation. The Vietnamese have two circular perimeters: An interior one keeping the GIs trapped, and an outer one keeping reinforcements out. As soon as they have called the information in, their helicopter is hit by a rocket propelled grenade and explodes in the air, killing everyone on board.

On the eighth day, the U.S. Army places a circular perimeter around the two Vietnamese perimeters, thinking that they have the Vietnamese surrounded. The Vietnamese then feign an attempted break out at one end of the perimeter. The U.S. Army concentrates its fire power on that end of the perimeter. But it is only a decoy, allowing the Vietnamese to escape by using previously dug tunnels at another end of the perimeter.

EPISODE XVI
I Don't Want to Kill Anyone

It's been a week since Ese's platoon has guarded the bridge. They have gotten back to their usual routine. Three Bears is increasingly worried because they have not had any contact with the enemy. He tells Ese when they are taking a short break on the trail, "I don't like it, Knucklehead."

"Don't like what?" asks Ese.

"Not having any contact with the enemy since we've been back in the bush."

"The less contact we have the better," says Ese.

"It's not that I like contact. It's not good because we become too lax, that's when all fuck will let lose," says Three Bears.

"I think you might have a point there."

The word is given to move out. Ese is walking point when he faintly hears and smells the enemy. He stops and signals for Cadillac and Da-Da to bring up their M-60 machine gun. The foliage is thick, which provides excellent cover for all combatants; although it can sometimes be an ally, or at other times an enemy.

When Da-Da and Cadillac reach Ese, Ese points to the left of the trail, indicating that's where the enemy is. They move stealthily. As they progress, the smell and noise become more distinct. Finally, they come to a point where they see five black-clad Viet Cong guerillas squatting around a fire, eating rice and fish. Ese hears movement behind him. He turns around and it is Three Bears and Marlon.

Three Bears indicates with his hand for them to take their positions and to fire when they hear his first round go off. Three Bears commences to shoot and the others follow. The Viet Cong are caught completely off guard. The bullets hit their bodies with such impact that they seem to temporarily fly. The five soldiers cease fire when they think all the soldiers are dead, then they promptly go to inspect them.

They find that all but one of the Vietnamese are dead. A female is wounded and seems to be dying. The soldiers look at one another thinking the same thing that Cadillac verbalizes, "Get it before it gets cold." Though all are tempted to rape the woman, no one does. Three Bears shoots her dead instead. An exalted feeling of accomplishment and vengeance fills the GIs, except for Marlon. Ese asks Marlon, "How come you didn't shoot?"

"No quiero matar a nadien. Nada más me quiero ir para casa," says Marlon without apology.

"What'd he say?" asks Cadillac.

"He says that he doesn't want to kill anyone. He just wants to go home," answers Ese.

"I no like to kill," says Marlon.

EPISODE XVII
The Hospital

Chuco gradually wakes up. He smells what seems like rubbing alcohol and pine scented disinfectant. The first thing he sees is a greenclothed figure with a shiny object on its chest. His legs feel numb. He begins to focus in on the object and discerns that it is a cross. Ya estuvo, that's it. They're giving me the last rites, he assumes.

"You have been unconscious for two days. You are going to be all right, son," says a middle-aged priest. "You are lucky that you didn't lose your legs. The doctor says that you will able to go back to your unit in a couple of weeks. Until then, rest so that your wounds can heal quickly." The priest does the sign of the cross and leaves.

Chuco is glad he is alive and as he falls asleep, he hears the familiar tranquil voice, "Te quiero…Te quiero un chingo…I quiero you…I love you."

Chuco feels a soft hand gently touching his shoulder to wake him. A handsome medic with a pleasant smile and masculine, yet affectionate voice tells him, "It's time for your medication, soldier. You've got to turn around so I can give you a shot in the rump." Chuco turns to his side and the medic sticks him with the needle.

"That didn't hurt much, did it?" asks the medic.

Chuco falls asleep and wakes the next day with a ravenous appetite. Standing over him is the medic with a tray of food on a cart. "I thought you'd wake up about now," says the medic, as he places the tray over Chuco's lap.

Chuco eats the bacon and eggs with relish and asks the medic, "What's your name?"

"They call me Biscuits."

"How come they call you that?"

"Because my buttocks look like biscuits," he says as he turns around and shows him his buttocks.

"I guess that's a good name, because they do look like biscuits," says Chuco with a grin.

"It's about time you get up and try to walk around. The doctors managed to get most of the shrapnel from your legs. It took about one hundred fifty stitches to sew you up, but you'll be well soon." Biscuits waits until Chuco finishes breakfast, then helps him up from bed.

"Hijo de la chingada," says Chuco, as he moves his legs from the bed to the floor. The medic assists him as he takes the first few tormenting steps. The trip to the showers is slow. Chuco thinks, Hijo de la chingada. Ahora sé como se siente mi abuelo con sus reumas en la mañana.[1] Chuco reaches the showers. Showering gives him a cleansing feeling.

The return trip to his bed is much easier. Chuco becomes more aware of his surroundings. Most of the patients are seriously wounded. Some lay unconscious and others are painfully awake. He passes one soldier whose legs and arms have been amputated. Next to him is a soldier whose face is completely bandaged, including his eyes. "What's wrong with these two guys?" he asks Biscuits staidly.

"The one with the missing legs and arms also lost his penis and testicles," whispers the medic. "The soldier with the bandaged face lost both of his eyes and most of his face. He's going to be transferred to Japan this afternoon. We don't think he's going to live."

"Pobre vatos.[2] I don't want to end up like that. I'd rather die," he hesitantly admits to Biscuits. As he speaks, two medics are placing a

---

1. Son of a whore. Now I know how grandpa feels with his rheumatism in the morning.
2. "Poor guys.

dead patient into a body bag.

After he is helped back into bed, he inspects the bed to his right. An overweight, middle-aged sergeant first class is breathing laboriously. "What happened to him?" he asks Biscuits.

"He got hit by mortars real bad. Tomorrow you're going to be transferred to another ward, where the patients are not so badly wounded. It won't be as bad as this," he reassures Chuco.

"I hope so. It ain't so good here."

Just as Biscuits had said, Chuco is transferred to another ward. The patient's wounds are not as exigent here. Several days later Chuco is feeling much better and is able to move around on crutches. Most of the patients are waiting for transfers to the United States or Japan.

Chuco is somewhat depressed and doesn't speak much to other patients. Occasionally, Biscuits comes around and plays gin rummy with Chuco. The afternoon before Chuco's release from his two week stay in the hospital, he is playing cards with Biscuits and asks him, "Have you ever been out in the field?"

"No, and I don't want to either. I didn't even want to come into the army. I tried to register as a conscientious objector, but I lost my case."

"Why did you do that?"

"Because I don't believe in violence or killing people. I believe in love, not hate. I'd rather help people and bring pleasure and joy to my fellow man."

The next day, Chuco is sent back to his unit's base camp where he waits for his company's return. He arrives in the early afternoon. It is scantly occupied by logistical and administrative personnel. He is assigned to the afternoon garbage detail. After signing in and leaving the headquarters building, he wonders, Why is it that it's mostly gabachos that work in the good jobs?

Chuco drives a lumbering, deuce and a half truck slowly from the mess hall to the dump. The dump is a deep and huge pit perpetually inundated by water and slop. On the way to the dump, dozens of Vietnamese tykes climb on the truck and scavenge for food. Like buzzard chicks, anything that they cannot use or eat, they toss off the truck. Chuco gets angry with them because whatever they litter, he must retrieve.

When he reaches the dump, he gets off of the truck and sees a long trail of rubbish. He walks to the rear of the truck and becomes so disquieted that he chucks one of the kids off of the truck, inadvertently throwing him into the pit. Without a second thought, Chuco jumps in the pit and pulls the kid out. Once out, he retches from the scum he has swallowed. He doesn't know whether to throw the kid back in or be glad the kid didn't drown. He drives back to the mess hall soaked in slime.

EPISODE XVIII
Basketball

Two weeks after the Vietnamese escaped, Machete's company is flown to the base of Landing Zone Hawk. They wait at the bottom because the company that is guarding the LZ is still on "the hill" as the GIs call it. The soldiers feel somewhat safer here than in the bush because of the fire support: Mortars and artillery which are placed on the hill.

Machete's company has suffered over sixty percent casualties. He abhors and loathes the Vietnamese more than ever. Here they are able to re-group physically and spiritually. But as always, they cannot let their defense down. Guards are on all sides of the perimeter. Most of the soldiers play cards, write letters, or lounge. Machete is seething with so much hate that he cannot sit and relax, so he volunteers to take one of the first guards.

A short while after he has taken his guard position, three Vietnamese men from the village down the road approach the perimeter and attempt to sell beer and sodas to the men.

"GI, GI number one. You number one," bawl the Vietnamese. "You buy cold beer or soda."

Machete becomes furious with the sight of the Vietnamese. He stands up from his position and mows down the Vietnamese with his machine gun. The Vietnamese fall dead. From now on, Machete is a pathological patriot.

Right before dawn, Landing Zone Hawk erupts like a volcano spewing artillery, mortars and machine gun fire. "We're being attacked. We're being attacked," a desperate voice says over the radio. The new company commander is not sure of what to do because this is his first time out in the bush and calls for Pepsi and a couple of other old-timers and asks them for advice.

"Have you tried to contact them?" Pepsi asks the new captain.

"Yes, but there's no answer."

"Hell, that ain't good. Look at all the mortars and rockets that are landing on those guys. It looks like the Fourth of July at the state fair in Omaha. Those guys are catching hell-fire. It looks like the small-arms fire is getting closer up the hill, meaning that the gooks are too close to our men, and artillery or gunships can't be called in because it'll be called in on our guys," calculates Pepsi.

"Shall we move out and try to help them?" asks the captain.

"I wish we could, captain. But since we can't communicate with them and tell them we're coming up, they won't know it's us and they'll shoot at us. I think it's better to wait until we can communicate with them, or until first light, so they can see that it's us coming up the hill. What we can do now is move as close as possible to the hill so we can be ready to move at dawn. We might even catch the gooks off guard," suggests Pepsi.

The captain takes Pepsi's advice. The GIs quickly depart toward the hill, with Machete walking point with his machine gun. They reach the bottom of the hill shortly before daylight. It is not long before they can head up toward the hill. The battle has been relentless and barbarous. By daybreak it subsides.

Machete leads the undermanned company up the hill. The Vietnamese are not expecting any opposition from the rear and Machete catches several Vietnamese off-guard and kills them. His entire body swells with exhilaration. Me los chingue. I fucked them up. I know they're going to hell because God doesn't like communists, he figures.

Just as Pepsi had surmised, the Vietnamese are not prepared for reinforcements so soon. Machete's company is able to shoo the Vietnamese off the hill. The enemy retreats from the opposite side of the hill that the GIs charged from.

When they reach the top of the hill, they witness a grisly scene of dead in disparate muddled contortions. Morning mist integrated with smoke from smoldering fires create a true-to-life cyclorama of war. Not one GI survived the attack.

Machete's company scours the hill for survivors. The only one they find is a semi-conscious North Vietnamese soldier with one foot half blown off. "Hey, Pepsi, look what I found," yells Dago Red, as he drags a young North Vietnamese soldier out from one of the bunkers. The adolescent soldier is terrified but does not cower; he knows that he is about to die. Like Machete, he too is a patriot, and willing to die for a cause.

Machete runs to Dago Red and says, "Just what I like. There's only one thing I like better than a dead gook, and that's a live one in my hands." He grabs the Vietnamese and stomps on his half-gone foot. The Vietnamese doesn't wince or quaver. "Oh, tough guy, huh? Un vato chingon. Just the way I like them," says Machete with a malefic grin.

Machete punches the prisoner in the stomach and chest. Again the Vietnamese does not demonstrate pain. "Yeah! So you really are a chingon. Bring his ass over there," he tells Dago Red, pointng to a pole for a makeshift basketball court. Many of the GIs have assembled around Machete and the prisoner. Dago Red drags the soldier to the pole. He ties his hands, feet and head to the pole.

The new captain realizes what's happening and rushes to intervene. "What's going on here, Sergeant Pepsi?" he inquires.

"Sir, I think you'd better go to the headquarters bunker and see if you can get hold of battalion," suggests Pepsi. The captain looks around the circle of hard-hearted and vindictive men. He correctly assumes that he'd better take Pepsi's advice, and smartly leaves for the command bunker.

"All right, lets play "guts" and see who has the most huevos. I'm first and I'm last," says Machete. Machete takes his bowie knife and superficially cuts the prisoner's left cheek, just enough to draw blood. Pepsi and some of the other soldiers have found some beer and hard liquor. They pass it around.

Pepsi rushes up to Machete and tells him, "Look what I found for you compadre…tequila!"

Machete grabs the tequila and takes a huge chug. Pepsi approaches the prisoner and Machete hands him the knife, and tells Pepsi, "Here's some gringo whiskey," handing him a fifth of whiskey. "Fucking-A Pepsi, it's your turn to work on the gook."

Pepsi guzzles some whiskey and prepares himself for the task at hand. All of the soldiers are now gathered around Machete, Pepsi and the prisoner. The first thing Pepsi does is gash the prisoners right cheek. This wound is deeper than the previous one and blood flows like liquid fire down the prisoners cheek. Then, he swiftly cuts off the right ear. The soldiers let out catcalls, whistles and cheers. Pepsi takes another drink and afterwards begins to yell, "Chingo. Chingo."

"Chingo. Chingo. Chingo," respond the soldiers.

Machete takes another deep gulp of tequila. He wipes his mouth with his arm, nonchalantly places his knife under the prisoners right eye and pokes the eye out. Most of the mutilated eye falls to the ground and the soldiers cheer. The soldier's eye drips tears of blood like Jesus Christ in the rose garden. Machete takes another swig of tequila. Then, he grabs the semi-conscious prisoner's head back and shoves the neck of the bottle into his throat until it is empty. "And don't say I never bought you a drink, asshole. Pepsi, Pepsi," shouts Machete while raising the bloody knife triumphantly. "Pepsi. Pepsi. Pepsi," Machete continues to incite the crowd. He raises his hands in the air, as if he is conducting an orchestra in full crescendo.

The soldiers are riled and motivated by Machete. "Pepsi. Pepsi. Pepsi," the soldiers chant over and over again in a frenzy.

Pepsi takes another drink of whiskey as the soldiers quiet down, they are in suspense as to what he is going to do next. The prisoner is conscious, but in shock, like a gazelle when a lioness has it by the throat. He feels minute pain.

Pepsi opens the prisoner's mouth, pulls the tongue out and cuts it off. Then he shoves it back into his mouth. The prisoner spits out the pink tongue, red with blood. To the amazement of the GIs, the prisoner does not cry out in pain. "Chingo. Chingo. Chingo," agitates Pepsi.

The soldiers yell hysterically, "Chingo. Chingo. Chingo."

Machete approaches the prisoner whose face is like a bloody Halloween mask. He tears the victim's shirt and pants off. He places the knife to the prisoner's midsection and cuts him open. His intestines bulge out like giant, hideous red and purple-hued worms. Then, he snatches a machete and shoves part of it up the soldier's anus. "Pepsi. Pepsi. Pepsi," again agitates Machete.

"Pepsi. Pepsi. Pepsi," rally the soldiers.

Pepsi senses that the victim is dying. "This is what you fuckers did to Rocket Man. So the payback's a motherfucker." Pepsi cuts off the prisoners testicles and penis, then stuffs them in the prisoner's mouth. The prisoner gives a sough of relief and dies.

The soldiers cheer, "Pepsi. Pepsi. Pepsi." Machete tells Pepsi to hold his hands out, then he washes the blooded hands with whiskey. "Pepsi won, motherfuckers," announces Machete, as he holds Pepsi's arm up like a referee in a boxing match.

Machete then cuts the piece of rope that is holding the prisoner's head up and the chin drops to his chest. He takes an extremely sharp machete and decapitates the prisoner. The head falls like a bowling ball. He picks up the head and says, "Chihuahua, this head is heavier than I thought." Then he throws it up with both hands toward the basket and the head falls through the hoop. "Two points, motherfuckers," he says malevolently.

The rest of the soldiers think Machete has come up with a great idea. They play "keep away" with the head and try to throw it through the hoop.

The next morning, the GIs gather their dead, load them on helicopters and abandon the LZ. The prisoner's body is left tied to the pole with his head piked on top. An ace of spades, the death card, has been stuck to his forehead as a warning to the enemy, which is a common scene of the war. Except this time, it is a North Vietnamese soldier, instead of a GI tied to the pole.

EPISODE XIX
Military Intelligence

Ese feels uneasy about working around villages out of free fire zones. In free fire zones, he doesn't have to worry about who he is firing at. If anything moves, he can kill it. The GIs have sayings such as: "Kick ass and take names later," or "If it's a dead gook, he's Viet Cong." Today, they are headed for a small village where Army intelligence has information that some of the villagers are Viet Cong. "I don't like going into these villages," he tells Three Bears, right before they are to enter the village.

"Me and you both," answers Three Bears.

"Anyways, military intelligence acts like they're so smart. It doesn't take a genius to figure out that these people don't want us here. A lot of them are Viet Cong. If these military intelligence people are so intelligent, they wouldn't be in the army in the first place," says Ese.

"You should know. You're the one who volunteered for the army and Viet Nam."

"I wouldn't do it again. But, it doesn't make any difference since we're both here now. Besides, I feel like the fucking border patrol when they used to stop us in the fields and ask us if we were citizens."

"Well, you'd better enjoy acting like one of them because when you get back home, they're going to stop you again," says Three Bears with a smirk.

"You got to be kidding. After all the hard work and shit I'm going through over here," says Ese flabbergasted.

"No matter what the fuck you do, Knucklehead, you're still a fucking greasy Mexican to the white man. So you'd better get used to it."

"How about you. You ain't nothing but a nasty Injun to the gringos."

"That's right. I'm only here because it was either this, or going to prison. And let me tell you, I don't like prison."

Cadillac is listening and adds, "Like Panther Man used to say, 'The Viet Cong never called me nigger.' He also used to say, 'This ain't our war. Our war's at home. When we get back on the block, we still ain't going to be nothing but nappy-headed niggers, along with the rest of the shithead greasers and spics, raggedy-ass honkies and blanket-ass-Indians.' "

"How come you guys fight so hard then?" asks Ese.

"Because if we don't, Charlie Cong will have our asses. We got to get him before he gets us. Besides, I don't mind killing a few motherfuckers once in a while," says Three Bears with satisfaction.

Their orders are to surround the village and check everyone's identification. If any of the village men start running, they are to use whatever necessary force to stop them.

They arrive at the small hamlet about midday. The sun hovers overhead like a colossal inferno. The villagers are caught off-guard. Women are nursing or cradling their babies. Children are gathered around an old man telling stories. Some men repair farm equipment while others lie in hammocks smoking tobacco. When they see the soldiers, three village men begin to run. They are shot dead.

A woman runs to one of the dead men and begins to wail over his body covered with a mixture of dust and blood. Ese and Three Bears walk over and try to pull her off. She resists. Ese and Three Bears are taken aback by her heinous stare of venomous malice. She pulls out a knife and lunges at Ese. Ese shoots her in the chest and kills her. Four small children without hands run to her and cry over her body lying in the dirt.

"Stupid puta. Why did she pull the knife and try to cut me? We weren't going to do nothing to her," he says with disgust.

"Go with the guys on the outer perimeter and forget about it, Knucklehead. She tried to kill us. Fuck the whore. This is a fucked up war and the only thing you have to remember is that you've got to stay alive. See those kids?" says Three Bears, pointing to the crying children gathered around their mother. "What do you think happened to their hands? You tell him, Beaucoup," he asks their Vietnamese advisor.

"Their hands were cut off by the VC last month because they took candy from some GIs and waved good-bye to them," says Beaucoup.

"This ain't the real world, Knucklehead. Don't feel any pity for the whore. I'll take care of the shit here. Remember, we got to go to the LZ so we can get resupplied and send your silly ass off for your week of rest and relaxation," says Three Bears.

"Relax. Fuck, I don't think I'll ever be able to relax again," says Ese with a simper. "I need a fucking beer, Bear."

Other than the four dead, the company does not encounter any other problems. They leave the village for a designated landing zone several kilometers away. For once, Ese does not volunteer for the point. The order is that if there is any enemy contact, they are to secure the area before they call in for resupply helicopters. When they reach their destination, they find several grass huts, or "hootches" as the GIs call them.

Ese and an FNG, a disparaging acronym that stands for "fucking new guy," inspect one of the huts. Ese is not concentrating and glances into the hut and doesn't see anything unusual. As Ese moves away from the hut, the excited FNG tells him, "There's a gook in the hootch."

"What?" asks Ese as he returns and looks in the hut. In a dark corner is a lethargic Vietnamese soldier lying in a hammock. Ese and the Vietnamese soldier look at each other, and then at two grenades laying on the floor. The Vietnamese attempts to reach for the grenades. But before he can grab the grenades, Ese shoots him with a full load of his nineteen round magazine. After he shoots him, Da-Da, Three Bears and Cadillac arrive and they continue to plug the soldier with bullets.

Three Bears lifts the dead soldier by the collar and the back of his pants and throws him out the door. The dead Vietnamese lands on his face inches in front of Ese's boots. His brains are grey in color and splatter all over Ese's boots. The platoon laughs. Ese laughs as well, but reflects, What the fuck's happening to me? This ain't funny. I wasn't like this a year ago.

"This is your lucky day, Knucklehead. You killed yourself a bitch. And now you've killed yourself a gook that couldn't move because it looks like he had malaria," Three Bears tells him. "Forget all this shit, because here comes your chopper. Have a good time with your buddies and drink some beer for me."

"You're right, Tres Osos. I got to get the fuck out of here," says Ese as he runs toward the helicopter. As the chopper lifts-off, Ese smiles and gives his comrades the finger and yells, "Fuck you, putos."

EPISODE XX
Pochos, Broncos, Manitos y Chuntaros

Chuco waits two days before the company arrives. He is overjoyed when he sees Ro-Ro and the rest of his platoon. Chuco has scrounged around the perimeter and obtained beer, liquor, marijuana, and cigarettes laced with opium. That evening after the platoon has cleaned-up and eaten barbecued steak, some soldiers bring out their guitars and play Mexican songs of love, honor and pride.

Chuco and Ro-Ro occasionally leave the circle of singing men to throw grenades outside the perimeter and shoot illumination flares in the air. This serves two purposes: one is to keep the enemy at bay and the other is to let out their frustrations. "Chinguen sus madres hijos de la chingada,"[1] yells Chuco as he throws a grenade.

When the mosquitoes become too aggressive, the soldiers retreat to their five man bunkers. The bunkers are made of old ammo boxes and sandbags. The soldiers sit inside the bunker drinking beer and smoking marijuana. After smoking marijuana, Chuco gets the urge to eat, and goes to his rucksack for some C-rations. He opens the rucksack and sees a healthy brown rat gnawing away at a can of ham and eggs or as the GIs call them, "ham and motherfuckers." "Está una pinche rata en mi rucksack,"[2] says Chuco, reaching for his rifle. "Le voy a dar en la madre."

"Nel loco. Dejala vivir,"[3] says Liebre as his ears become livid. "Amara el rucksack y trampa la. Y luego le damos corte."

"Si, está bien Liebre," concurs Ro-Ro.

"Corte! Estan babosos. The fucking rata me estaba jambando mi

---

1. "Go fuck your mamas, son of a bitches,"
2. "There's a fucking rat in my rucksack"
3. "I'm going to kill it,"
   "Don't slick. Let it live,"

refin. Ya le hizo un hoyo al bote de gallina que me mandó mi jefita,"[4] answers Chuco closing the rucksacks drawstring. The rat squeals and screeches. Chuco opens the rucksack and hits the rat with the butt of his rifle hard enough to knock it out, but not to kill it.

"Símon loco,[5] who are we to condemn this rata. Nada más está haciendo lo que estamos haciendo nosotros. El son-of-a-biche tiene que comer y sobrevivir, igual que todos,"[6] says Ro-Ro, defending the rat.

"Símon que yes,"[7] says Liebre, with his eyes sparkling from the opium laced marijuana. "Se vale lo que hizo la rata porque todos chiriamos, compa."[8]

"O.K., pero al jodido lo pescamos. And he has to pay," answers Chuco. "Igual cuando we catch a gook y le damos en la madre.[9] Or when they catch one of us, ellos no nos pasan quebrada."[10]

"Sure, carnal. But we all have cuetes[11] to defend ourselves. Está rata no tiene nada mas que unos dientes amarillos,"[12] says Ro-Ro with sarcasm.

"Esa mordida que te da the fucking rata can give you rabies y puedes tirar la vuelta,"[13] says Chuco.

"Yo digo que he should die," says Chuco.

"Que chingue su madre la pinche rata, hija de su chingada madre.

---

4. "Tie up the rucksack and trap it. Then we'll give him a trial
   "Yes, Liebre is right," concurs Ro-Ro.
   "A trial! Your nuts. The fucking rat was swiping my grub. He's already mad a hole in the canned chicken my mom sent me,"
5. "Right slick,
6. "It's doing the same thing we are. The son of-a-bitch has to eat and survive, just like everyone else,"
7. "Yes, that's right,"
8. "It's right what the rat did because we all cheat, buddy."
   "O.K., but we caught him.
9. "Just like when we catch a gook and fuck him up.
10. they don't give us a break."
11. guns
12. "This rat only has a few yellow teeth,"
13. "That fucking rat bite can give give you rabies and you can kick the bucket,"

Que muera la puta,"[14] shouts Patillas in drunken condemnation.

"Bueno, votamos, qué no,"[15] says Ro-Ro.

"Why not. Let's vote. This rata ain't worth fighting over. Ain't that right, vato nuevo,"[16] says Chuco winking his eye and turning to the new recruit and fifth man in the bunker.

"Yo soy nuevo aquí [17] and I don't know nothing. I just got here from Arisa," [18] says the new guy shyly.

"I say he's got to die," says Chuco.

"Ay tú, ya comensates con tu pinche Inglés, pinche pocho culero. Mexicano falso," [19] says Ro-Ro.

"Fuck you, Ro-Ro. If anybody is a Mexicano falso it's you. What are you doing fighting under the gabacho flag, if you're a Mexican citizen. Anyway, you ain't nothing but a chuntaro."

"Estoy aquí a por que los gooks mataron ami hermano. Y me quiero matar algunos de ellos."

"Calma, Calma huercos chocantes. Yo digo que le debemos de dar una quebrada," says Liebre.

"¿Que sabes tu? Tejano tonto," says Patillas. "Yo digo que le demos de dar en la torre."

"Órale. Manito huero pendejo. De donde sales que los Tejanos son tontos," answers Liebre. "A poco los de Nuevo Mexico son muy listos."

"Símon, síquiera no semos patas rajadas indios como los broncos de Tejas."

"Guacha le hay Patillas. Porque yo soy indio," [20] says Ro-Ro. The alco-

---

14. "I say it should die,"
    "Fuck the rat up. The whore should die,"
15. "Well, let's vote,"
16. new guy,"
17. "I'm new here
18. Arizona,"
19. "There you go with your stupid English, you Mexican traitor,"
20. hillbilly."
    "I'm here because the gooks killed my brother. And I want to kill some of them."
    "Be calm, be calm, you annoying billy goats. I say we should give him a break," *Footnote continued on next page.*

hol and the stress of combat is taking a toll on them. They are increasingly hostile to one another.

"Entonces tú también eres baboso," [21] answers Patillas as he gets up close to Ro-Ro and plants his finger on his chest. He is bigger and stronger than Ro-Ro, but Ro-Ro relies on his heart for fighting.

Chuco also gets up and tells Patillas, "Chale vato, no le hagas así a Ro-Ro," [22] Chuco warns Patillas.

"Esto no está bien que ustedes huercos paquetien, y le brinquen a Patillas," [23] says Liebre defending Patillas.

In anger, Patillas shoves Ro-Ro. He falls backward and knocks over a white-gas lamp made with C-ration cans, with a piece of cloth as a wick. Luckily, the gas spills away from the soldiers. It spreads like a swift wind on the floor. The soldiers swoop their rifles and bottles up and run out like fleeing impalas. Chuco panics when his shirt is caught by concertina wire which surrounds the bunker. He can't pull loose, so he takes off his shirt and runs away from the burning bunker.

They run to an adjacent bunker and hide behind it. A lucid full moon exhales illuminated gray rays. "No saquen las cabezas porque van a comenzar a explotar las balas," [24] says Ro-Ro. Within moments, the bullets whiz out of the bunker in all directions. Illumination flares are shot in the air. The rat that was inside the bunker scampers in front of them with a piece of cracker in his mouth. The five soldiers

---

20. "What do you know? You dumb Texan," says Patillas. "I say we
   should do him in."
   "Hey. Stupid little light skinned brother. Where do you come
   off that Texans are stupid," answers Liebre. I suppose the New
   Mexicans are real smart."
   "Yeah, that's right. At least we aren't bare footed Indians like
   the wild people from Texas."
   "Watch it Patillas. Because I'm an Indian too,"
21. "Then you're stupid too,"
22. "Hey dude, don't do that to Ro-Ro,"
23. "It's not right that you dudes gang up on Patillas,"
24. "Don't stick your heads out because the bullets are going to start
   exploding,"

look at one another and laugh.

"Que vivan los chuntaros,"[25] says Chuco, lifting a bottle of whiskey.

"Que vivan," say the others, in concert, lifting their bottles and taking a drink.

"Que vivan los Pochos,"[26] says Ro-Ro with a big smile.

"Que vivan," say the others taking another drink.

"Que vivan los Tejanos broncos,"[27] says Patillas with a shit-faced grin.

"Que vivan," they all respond, and take another drink.

"Que vivan los Manitos,"[28] says Liebre, his green eyes glistening in the moonlight.

"Que vivan," they all say again.

After they take a drink, Chuco notices that the new guy from Arizona seems dejected. "Y que vivan los vatos de Arisa,"[29] yells Chuco, so the new soldier can feel as part of the group.

"Ajúa," shouts Liebre. "Y que viva la raza,"[30] taking another drink.

By now, the bullets in the bunker have been expended. Everyone on that side of the perimeter is watching the bunker burn. In the bunker next to them, some black soldiers talk about the situation. "What's happening?" asks one soldier.

"You're a new dude, but you'll get to know some of them boys. It's them crazy chingos. Those are some crazy essays in that platoon. Every time they get to drinking and smoking dew, they start playing guitars, singing and shouting. Then a little while later they gets to arguing, and then a little bit later, they gets to fighting," answers a soldier.

"Those are some partying motherfuckas," says a second soldier. "In the morning, they'll all get up real early and go out on patrol as if

---

25. "Long live the Mexican hillbillies,"
26. "Long live the traitor Mexicans,"
27. "Long live the wild Texans,"
28. "Long live the little brothers,"
29. "And long live the guys from Arizona,"
30. "Long live the Mexicans,"

nothing happened. But this time, them motherfuckas fucked up by burning that bunker down. That's sergeant Row-Row's bunker, the craziest motherfucker you ever want to meet. He's got two bronze stars and a silver star…except he gets busted just about every month, then he makes sergeant again about a month later. I don't even know what his rank is now."

"When all the caps start busting, that's one motherfucker you want on your side, 'cause that crazy fucker got a whole lot of balls and he won't leave you behind. I heard he volunteered for the Nam cause the gooks kilt his brother and he wants to get even with them. But I do know that him and our Mr. Charley captain don't get along. Row-Row better be careful because Mr. Charley is going to send him to Long Binh Jail."

"Sho' enough, he would like to send him to LBJ," says a third soldier. "But Mr. Charley better watch out for that Row-Row, too. Because Row-Row will kill him first chance he gets. I'd like to kill Mr. Charley myself, cuzz. I hopes Row-Row kills that cracker, chuck, motherfucka cause Mr. Charley don't like brothers no way."

The third soldier adds, "That's right youngster, Mr. Charley captain has done bloods wrong, big time. When I was a new motherfucka, just like you, a new baby, I seen these dead brothers kilt and shot up. Must of been twenty-five wooley-headed dead niggas piled up on ones another. They was over there in the middle of the perimeter," he turns around and points to the helicopter landing pad. "There was a couple of homeboys that lived and they said that Mr. Charley sent them into an ambush on purpose.

By the time I seen the brothers, the blood had done turned black and caked on them. And that ain't the first time it's happened in the Nam. Some other cracker, peckerwood, motherfucker officers have sent bloods off to get kilt. That's why a whole lots of brothers don't walk no point no mo'."

When the flames of the bunker die down, mortars begin to fall on the perimeter. "Incoming," yell some of the soldiers. All the soldiers rush inside their bunkers. Chuco is last to reach the door of the bunker. As he takes a step inside, a mortar explodes behind him and he feels some brief pain, then blacks out.

EPISODE XXI
Parranda/Binge

At the airport at Chu Lai, Ese walks off the C-130 Eagle feeling at ease. Though he feels somewhat apprehensive about not having his rifle, which was taken away before he boarded the airplane, he is glad that he is out of the bush. He, Chuco and Machete were supposed to meet in Da Lat, a Vietnamese resort area. They had decided, by writing one another, that it would be better to stay in country rather than to take their one week of rest and relaxation outside Viet Nam. They have decided on this because they knew that if they left Viet Nam, they may desert and go home.

When Ese called from his company headquarters to Chuco's company area, he was informed that Chuco was in a Da Nang hospital recovering from shrapnel wounds. "Da Nang? What the hell is he doing way up there?" He was told that there wasn't enough room for him in Saigon, and that they had to transfer him north to Da Nang.

Ese then called Machete's company headquarters and he was informed that Machete hadn't arrived from the field. He left a message for Machete instructing him to stay put and that he would fly up to see him. Ese figured that he'd take a plane to Chu Lai and meet with Machete, then they'd take a plane to Da Nang from there. He knew that he wouldn't have trouble flying around the country because all they had to show was their orders, and if there was room on a plane, they could board it. Chu Lai is headquarters of the 23rd Infantry Division—the Americal Division. It is a huge military installation of several square miles.

From the terminal building, Ese walks outside and reconnoiters the surroundings. A multitude of soldiers move in and out of the terminal.

Some soldiers are ferried on trucks or buses while others have personal jeeps. Ese observes two medics park a medic-jeep with Red Cross markings several meters from him. The jeep is equipped with litter racks fitted behind the driver's and front passenger's seat. The medics get off the jeep and walk inside the terminal. Ese walks to the jeep and gets in. Since military vehicles are started by switches, not keys, he doesn't have any difficulty in starting the jeep and driving away.

The first thing he wants to do is find a liquor store or package store as they are called in the army. By asking for directions from pedestrians, Ese has little difficulty locating the package store. He thinks, "I almost feel like a civilian by getting off the vehicle and going to a liquor store. He spends all his money on two bottles of tequila and a case of beer. The bulk of his monthly two hundred-forty dollar pay he sends home to his mother. As he gets into the jeep, a tough looking major with sneering eyes, walks up to the side of Ese's jeep and asks him, "What are you doing with that jeep, soldier, you don't seem to be a medic? You look more like an infantryman that belongs out in the bush."

Knowing well that military courtesy does not approve of saluting when sitting, Ese salutes the major with his left hand while he sits in the driver's seat. Then in broken English, performing his dumb Mexican act, he says, "I no spic too mush Inglish, ser. I in hoss-pitel. I go back to boosh mañana. Medicks sends me for bier. I not know to mush."

"Stupid Mexican," says the major shaking his head in disgust. You don't even speak English. Well, at least you're going back to the bush tomorrow. All right then, but make sure you do. I don't want to see you around here anymore, comprenday?"

"Si, señor," replies Ese as he salutes again with his left hand. He puts the jeep in reverse and intentionally jerks it in stops and starts to make it seem like he doesn't know how to drive. He finally pulls out and turns the jeep so that it taps the major and knocks him down. Then he straightens out the jeep and drives away.

The major gets up furiously dusting himself and screams, "You stupid, dumb Mexican! Don't you know how to drive? They ought to send all you people back to Mexico."

Ese smiles with his anima glowing and says to himself, "Pinche gringo, baboso." [1] He feels great. He snatches a beer and thinks, "Now, to find that puto, Machete." He takes out a cassette player from his knapsack, turns it on and plays his favorite song, "Quiero Que Sepas," [2] by Los Gavilanes del Norte. "Quiero que soples," [3] he sings along.

He chooses a soldier walking along the road to ask where Machete's unit is quartered. "Hey buddy, where is the First-of-the-Forty-sixth of the One Ninety-sixth?"

"Over there. The second turn to your right," he says rigidly pointing to his right.

"Wow, that gringo looked pale and dead enough to be an escapee from the morgue," murmurs Ese to himself. He goes to where he was directed. He finds Machete's company area and drives his jeep to another company area several meters away to avoid suspicion. Before he walks away, he inspects the jeep and finds a first-aid pouch underneath the passenger's seat. He opens the pouch and Ese's eyes become buoyant and huge. "A la chingada, I hit the jackpot," he says to himself, picking up two vials of morphine. "I can sell this shit to somebody."

He puts the vials underneath the passenger's seat and saunters off to Machete's company. He finds the orderly room, walks in and takes

1. "Stupid fucking gringo."
2. "I Want You to Know"
3. "I want you to blow,"

off his hat. "May I help you, soldier?" asks a clerk sitting behind a desk.

"Well, ain't this the shits! You're the same guy that took our orders in Oakland, aren't you?"

"Yes, I was in Oakland a few months back. But you look just like all the other guys in green. May I help you?" he asks with indifference.

Gringo sangron y salado.[4] He's still got bad breath and dandruff, thinks Ese. "I'm looking for a friend of mine He was supposed to come in yesterday from the bush for his R&R."

"There is only one soldier that came in yesterday. Is he a bullet-headed soldier that everyone calls Macheti?"

"That's him, Jim."

The clerk motions with his right hand, "As you walk out the door, turn to your left. It's the second building to your right," says the clerk. "I hope you're taking him away because last night he was causing all kinds of commotion. He wouldn't let me sleep. He didn't settle down until the MPs came and threatened to take him away."

"Thanks a lot, buddy," says Ese, using courtesy to mask his sarcasm. Gabacho baboso,[5] he thinks. Ese goes to the building and finds Machete sitting on his bunk, cleaning his M-60 machine gun. "Órale! pinche[6] Machete," shouts Ese.

Machete looks up and is jubilant to see Ese. The first thing Ese says is, "I need a beer." They speak to one another as if they had just seen each other the previous day. They don't shake hands because their spiritual bonding does not need to be demonstrated physically.

"I got some cold ones in this ice canister," says Machete, opening a canister full of beer lying in a bed of ice. He opens a beer with a can opener and hands it to Ese.

Ese grabs it and finishes it in one long drink. "Man, that was good.

---

4. "Dour and snobbish gringo.
5. "Stupid white man,"
6. "Hey fucking

Are you ready to go? I have a jeep that I borrowed from some medics. Our plans have changed because Chuco is wounded and is in a Da Nang hospital."

"¿Como está, se lo chingaron gacho?" asks Machete.

"Esta bien[7], he'll be out in a couple of weeks. I figure we can drive to Da Nang instead of flying, so we can party hard."

"That sounds good to me. Esperate un poquito.[8] I just got one thing to do, y luego nos descuentamos.[9] I got to go see my caramiada,[10] Loco. He's got some grifa that he's going to give me. Esta en Charlie company playing cards con unos Puerto Riqueños."[11] Machete goes to his wall locker and pulls out an M-16, a bandolier of magazines, a holstered forty-five pistol, and hands them to Ese. "Here, take these. It's a present."

"Like they used to say in the old movies: 'Gee!, this is swell. This is jake,' " says Ese, smiling while strapping on the forty-five. "I always wanted to wear a gun like Hopalong Cassidy or the Cisco Kid. Y si te portas bien,[12] you can be Jingles or Poncho."

Machete picks up his gear and M-60 machine gun and says, "Vamonos. No has cambiado nada. Todavia estas igual…igual de pendejo."[13]

"I'll drink to that," says Ese, after quickly quaffing another beer and following Machete's example of stuffing beer into his large pants' pockets. Along the way to Loco's location, Ese and Machete gabber about the letters they've received and about things back home.

They pass a long line of sleeping quarters and company headquar-

---

7. "How is he. Did they fuck him up bad?"
   "He's all right,
8. Wait a little bit.
9. then we can split.
10. piss-faced friend
11. He's in Charlie company playing cards with some Puerto Ricans."
12. And if you act right,
13. Let's go. You haven't changed a bit, your still as dumb as ever."

ters. They are painted in the standard olive-drab, army color. Each building sleeps twenty men. Because of the heat, the top half of the walls are made of screen wire with wooden shutters that can be lifted or closed shut when the need arises.

As they get closer to where Loco is, salsa music becomes louder. "Here's the place," says Machete, as he walks into the billets.

Ese walks in and sees five soldiers drinking beer, playing cards, and speaking in Spanish. After Machete introduces Ese to the soldiers, Ese says, "Tengo que ir a tirar el agua."[14] He leaves in haste for the latrine.

When he reaches the latrine, he jumps up and down trying not to urinate in his pants. He unzips his fly just in time to pee in the urinal. "Ah, that feels good," he says while he relieves himself. After he finishes, he zips up his pants; and since he is not circumcised, catches the foreskin of his penis in the zipper. "Fuck that hurts," says Ese in horrible pain. He has done this before. He knows that the only way to get loose is to hold the foreskin as well as possible with one hand, and yank the zipper down quickly with his other hand. He jerks the zipper down and almost lets out a scream of agony. "Man, that hurts," he murmurs.

When Ese gets back to the billets, Machete is arguing with one of the Puerto Rican soldiers. "Entonces tú estas diciendo que ustedes son mejores que nosotros, porque no hablamos como ustedes," says Machete angrily.

"A cual español. Los mexicanos no saben hablar,"[15] answers the Puerto Rican soldier, equally angry as he pulls out a small pocket knife.

"Oh shit," says Ese. "A fight." Loco and the other soldiers intervene and calm things down. They continue playing cards.

---

14. "I've got to take a leak,"
15. "Then your saying you're better than us because we don't speak like you do,"
   "What Spanish. Mexicans don't know how to speak,"

Machete then asks the soldier with the knife to let him inspect it. He hands Machete the knife, and Machete mockingly begins cleaning his finger nails with it. "Dame la navaja,"[16] demands the owner, putting out his hand.

"Aqui está tu pinche navaja, puto,"[17] says Machete as he stabs the soldier in the palm.

When the knife goes clean through his hand, he screams in pain, "Hijo de puta."

"Chingate, hijo de la chingada. Puerto Riqueño baboso."[18]

The other Puerto Ricans are offended and stare menacingly at Machete. Machete reacts by firing three bullets to the ceiling. "Vamonos, a la verga,"[19] says Ese, pointing his rifle at the soldiers. Ese, Loco and Machete back away towards the door and leave.

"Y ya no regresen, mexicanos locos,"[20] barks one of the soldiers from inside the billets.

"Y decen que yo estoy loco,"[21] says Loco as they walk away.

"Let's go to the jeep," says Ese.

"Bueno, yo voy para el club. Que les vaya bien[22] and I'll see you when you get back," says Loco, handing Machete a pouch of marijuana in a brown paper bag.

"Gracias Loco, hay nos guachamos en una semana,"[23] says Machete. When they reach the jeep he compliments Ese, "Te aventates,[24] Ese. Look at this jeep; it even has a canvas top just in case it rains."

"As the sheepherder would say, 'Let's get the flock out of here,'"

---

16. "Give me the knife,"
17. "Here's your fucking knife,"
18. Go get fucked, Puerto Rican son-of-a-bitch."
19. "Let's get the fuck out,"
20. "And don't come back you crazy Mexicans,"
21. "And they say I'm crazy,"
22. "All right, I'm going to the club. Good luck
23. "Thanks Loco, we'll see you in a week,:
24. "You done good,

says Ese before he tilts a can of beer to his mouth. "Watch this, vato, I can even make this jeep spin-out." He jerks the clutch and guns the accelerator, leaving a ball of dust behind him.

Before they leave the base, he tells Machete, "Necesitamos hielo para la birria[25] before we split. Let me pull over to that company area over there," says Ese, pointing to a group of buildings to his right. He drives the jeep up to one of the buildings and tells Machete as he gets off the jeep, "This looks like a mess hall. Look at all the flies hanging around the door. Guacha el[26] jeep and I'll go see if I can secure some ice." Ese gets off the jeep and struts to the mess hall.

When he walks in through a side entrance of the mess hall, a skinny white cook sees him and asks in a Texas drawl, "What the fuck do you want here, Poncho?"

Ese becomes agitated but remains calm. "Our unit is TDY down the road for a couple of months. Our mess sergeant, Sergeant Chingaderas, talked to your MMFIC, a certain Sergeant Wilson or Williams or something like that, about us securing some ice from you people.

"We do have a Sergeant Williams and what in tarnation is an MMFIC?"

"Oh, that stands for the Main-Mother-Fucker-In-Charge," says Ese, laughing."

"Get the fuck out of here, Meskin. Who in the hell do you think you're talking to?"

"You need some weed? We can trade."

"Are you crazy? We're up to our ass in grass."

"Morphine?" asks Ese.

The cook's piss-green eyes light up. "Morphine! How much you got,

25. "We need ice for the beer
26. Watch the

124

asshole?"

"I got a vial."

"How much you want for it?"

"I figure it's worth about one hundred dollars. But, I'll let you have it for..." says Ese as he scans the kitchen, "forty dollars, plus two boxes of heat tabs, four cases of C-rations, and six cases of beer and say, enough ice to fill our OD canister."

"That's a lot of stuff."

"Quit bullshitting, gringo. You know that stuff ain't yours, so quit fucking around."

"All right. But I've got to see the shit first," says the cook, giving in.

"I'll be right back," says Ese. He returns to the jeep and is elated when he tells Machete, as he takes another beer, "Look under your seat and hand me a pouch that's there."

Machete puts his hand under the seat and pulls out an olive-drab pouch. "What the fuck is this?" he asks.

"Morphine. I've got this stupid gabacho-junkie on the line," he says after gulping the beer.

"Where did you get this shit?"

"From this magic jeep," Ese says, laughing. "En un poquito,[27] we're going to get some pisto, forty pesos[28] and some C-rations. I'll be right back."

Ese walks back to the mess hall and tells the cook, "O.K., puto, I've got the shit. Let me see the money."

"Here's the forty dollars, Poncho."

"Fuck you." Ese is livid and takes the money. He calms himself, eases his grip on his M-16 and asks "Where's the beer and the rest of the shit?"

---

27. "In a little bit
28. booze, forty dollars

"In the supply room. Bring your jeep over around the back, and we'll load it up."

Ese steps out the door and signals Machete to bring the jeep. They load the provisions and leave the compound. The cook watches them leave. Ese throws him the finger and yells, "Go fuck your mama, asshole." The morphine has taken effect and the cook is oblivious to the taunts.

Machete and Ese play their favorite music as they cruise along, just as they had done eight months ago in Illusion. The only difference is that now they are soldiers in a war and ten thousand miles away from home.

Driving down Highway One, they see postcard sceneries of rice paddies, water buffalos, grass huts and black-clad farmers. Children scurry on rice paddy dikes carrying water and food for the farmers. Alongside the road, antiquated men and women carry heavy baskets on poles in an ancient, Asian, methodological trot.

After a couple of hours of driving, Ese pulls over so they can relieve themselves of the beer they have imbibed. Ese gets off the jeep unpoised with an opium-laced marijuana cigarette in his mouth. As he urinates, he tells Machete, "Man, that sure feels good. Do you smell something dead? It smells worse than a dead skunk. I bet there's a dead vato around here somewhere."

While Ese is talking, Machete walks to a tree surrounded by a clump of bushes. He calls for Ese and tells him as he points. "Mira, there's a dead gook."

Ese struts to Machete and sees a dead Viet Cong soldier hanging naked and upside down by a rope tied to his left ankle. "How long do you think that son-of-a-bitch has been hanging there?" asks Ese.

"I don't know, but probably for a few days because look at all the maggots on his face."

"Mira, there's even maggots coming out of his culo. I wonder what happened to his dick?"

"Somebody probably cut it off to show the rest of the gooks what will happen to communists," says Machete.

"Or maybe somebody cut off his weenie because it was bigger than his own and wants to fuck his old lady with it." They both laugh as they head for the jeep.

After driving for several miles, Ese asks, "How does it look on the map?"

Machete picks up a map and tells Ese, "We should be about three miles from the next compound. "Look up ahead. It looks like an army jeep is stuck in the mud. Let's stop and see what we can do."

Ese does what Machete requests. He pulls up to a swarthy, white soldier and a light-skinned black one and asks, "What the fuck's the problem, fellas?"

"Shit-bitch-dog-motherfucker!" says the white soldier. "If you guys will hook our chain to your jeep, you can pull us out."

"We can do that," says Machete. "Let's get off and help them."

"Fuck no…bullshit. I ain't doing no manual work! I'm on vacation."

Machete laughs and gets off the jeep. After the truck is pulled out, the black soldier tells them, "Thanks a lot, bros'. We appreciate your help."

"That's right," adds the white soldier.

"Where can we get a piece of ass around here?" asks Ese.

"Follow us. It's a little red hootch-bar on the right-hand side of the vill," answers the black soldier.

"Where you from in the world anyway, bleed? asks Ese, teasing the black soldier.

"I'm from L.A."

"Does that stand for lower Alabama or what, eh?" says Ese laughing.

"You're about a jive motherfucker. Follow us before it gets dark and the Military Police or VC start fucking with you," warns the black soldier.

"Fuck the MPs, fuck the VCs and fuck your mamas," says Ese as he stands up in the jeep grabbing his crotch with his right hand and holding his M-16 up in the air with his left hand. "Me los chingo, [29] dudes." With that said, he sits back and drives off in a huff. "Fuck those queer-rear-echelon-punk-motherfuckers. Fucking REMF assholes," he tells Machete, as they shriek with laughter.

"Man, those are some crazy Meskins. You know they're asking for trouble," says the black soldier as he watches Ese and Machete drive away.

Ese and Machete are exhilarated at the thought of meeting some prostitutes.

"Just don't eat that shit, or your lips will fall off," cautions Machete.

"Just give me a couple of more beers, and I think I can play the harmonica on those dink putas," says Ese, cupping his hands, simulating performing cunnilingus sideways. "The good thing about eating these gook putas is that they don't have too much panocha[30] hair, so you don't have to worry about getting some stuck between your teeth."

"Fuck. I'd never eat none of that gook shit. You know how much I hate the motherfuckers. I'm just doing it cause I haven't had nalga[31] in eight months," says Machete.

Ese and Machete are going to make the most of the R&R because they know this probably is the only time they will be able to gallivant in Viet Nam. It doesn't take them long to reach their destination. Ese parks the jeep in front of a makeshift hovel constructed of cardboard, flattened cans and old ammunition boxes.

29. "I'll fuck them up,
30. pussy
31. ass

"I wonder if this is the place?" asks Machete.

"As Curly Q. Links of the Three Stooges would say: 'If there's no other place around the place, this must be the place.' Yeah stupid, it's the only red-painted shack in the whole place."

"Fuck, this is a raggedy place," complains Machete.

"Don't worry about it. It's O.K. as long as we get fucked. I sure do feel good. This is the best I've felt since I've been in Nam."

"Well, don't get too comfortable. Remember, we're surrounded by gooks," warns Machete.

"No shit, Sherlock. Take it easy, Machete. Y que chinguen sus madres los Vietnamese. Let's throw party," says Ese, buckling his forty-five pistol around his waist and locking and loading his M-16. Though they don't demonstrate it, they are leery of the increased vicissitudes of dealing with Vietnamese who are not in free fire zones. Nonetheless, they are urged on by their sex drives and reckless audacity.

"¡Órale, cabrones!" [33] yells Ese, walking into the bar with Machete behind him.

Swiftly, three gaunt, yet curvaceous bar girls, turn toward Ese and Machete. One of them hollers out, "Messikens, Messikens," and runs to Ese and grabs his crotch. "I like Messiken."

"Shit, ruca, take it easy, that hurts," says Ese. "How do you know we're Mexicans anyway?"

"We see TV. We see cowboys…we see Messikens in movie. We like Messikens. Same, same Vietnamese," she says, placing her arm next to his, comparing skin pigmentation.

"Bullshit!" says Machete. "We don't look like no kind of gooks."

Ese grins and thinks, Machete can sure pass for some kind of gook.

Like a bird of prey, Machete visually reconnoiters the bar and spots

---

33. "Watch out shitheads!"

a pusillanimous Vietnamese man lying on his stomach on a table towards the back of the bar. He promptly goes to him. The Vietnamese has been wounded by shotgun pellets in the back. He is terrified when Machete points his M-16 to his face. Machete's eyes scintillate with such hate and ferocity, that even the devil would be impressed.

"Don't shoot, GI. GI no shoot," pleads the Vietnamese.

"Wait, wait a minute," calls out Ese, observing what is happening.. He rushes to Machete. "Take it easy, maliseala," he says as he gently lowers the barrel of Machete's M-60 machine gun. "If you shoot this motherfucker, it's for sure we aren't going to get any culo. The MPs will come around and all sorts of pedo[34] will start. Think about it, Machete. Let me take care of this. Give us three beers," he asks the proprietor while holding up three fingers.

Ese then asks the wounded man, "What happened to you, asshole? You were around the army compound last night, huh, motherfucker? My friend here is going to shoot you."

"No, no, VC shoot me. I hate VC. VC number ten. GI number one."

"Well here is a beer anyway, asshole," Ese tells him as he hands him a beer that the proprietor has brought. "Look here, puto," says Ese, pointing the M-16 to the man's forehead. "Keep coming around the compound and my friend here is going to shoot you dead. It's better if we get the fuck out of here."

The proprietor helps the man get up from the table and leads him out the rear exit.

"I don't trust any kind of gook motherfuckers. Let's screw these putas and get the fuck out of here," says Machete with rancor.

"All right, but only one of us can go to the room and screw these putas. Let's flip for it."

---

34. shit

"Sure," says Machete, pulling out a coin and flipping it. "Call it in the air."

"Tails." The coin lands heads. "How come you always win?" grumbles Ese.

They go and sit at a table. The bar girls quickly converge on them. The one that initially grabbed Ese sits on his lap.

"Shit, look at these rucas. They're dirtier than shit. I guess it doesn't make any difference, 'cause at least they're rucas. Anyways, they aren't any scummier than some of the whores you used to screw back in Illusion."

"Me! Only me!," exclaims Ese incredulously, shaking his head. "How about Dirtbomb? You almost married the whore." Ese then mischievously snatches the head of the girl sitting on his lap and shakes her head close to the table. Lice fall out of her hair and onto the table. Ese takes the handle of his pistol and pounds on the lice.

By this time, other Vietnamese have gathered around, knowing well that where there are GIs, there is money or food. When Ese pounds the lice, people laugh heartily and enjoy his antics. "Machete, before you go to the room, deja bailar un borle con esta ruca?" [35] he asks. He pulls the girl up from her seat and turns on his cassette player full blast, and dances Norteño style to "Quiero Que Sepas." "This ruca dances O.K. for a gooka," he yells to Machete. Ese closes his eyes and fantasizes that he is dancing with Muñeca.

One of the girls sitting next to Machete salaciously rubs his crotch. "Boom-boom, GI, number one boom-boom. We go sucky-fucky. Short-time." She feels Machete's erection and says, "GI ready. I make Messikin baby for you papa-san."

"Fuck you, puta. I don't want no gook babies."

Ese finishes dancing and goes back to the table. "I'm taking this

---

35. let me have a dance with this chick?"

whore to the room," says Machete getting up. "Here, take my sixty and I'll take your sixteen. It's better if you pull guard with it out here."

"Don't take too long, so I can have my turn too carnal. Then we can get the flock out of here. Looks like you got company," says Ese, pointing to two malnourished tykes following Machete.

"Vamonos a la chingada. Get the fuck out of here you little bastards."

"No, no they my little brother. They afraid to be alone. Please let them stay by the door," pleads the girl.

"Fuck, all right," agrees Machete as lust overwhelms his contempt.

Entering the room the girl asks, "Five dalla, MPC, you pay now."

"Wait , if you give me good short-time, I'll give you ten dollars MPC when we finish."

"No, no. You give me money now."

"Fuck it then, puta, I'll get me another bitch," says Machete.

"Sure papa-san, we fuck first," says the girl, giving in because she and her brothers have not had anything to eat for days.

She leads Machete to a bedbug infested, U.S. Army cot and disrobes. Machete doesn't take his pants off, he just pulls them down below his knees. He mounts the girl with his M-16 in his hand. As he is about to penetrate the girl, he senses something touching his legs. He turns around and sees the girl's brothers trying to lift his wallet.

"Get the fuck out of here, you little bastards," he says scowling. The kids retreat, but only to try and lift his wallet again when he mounts the girl. Once more, he becomes angry and shoos them away. This goes on a few more times, until Machete becomes so exasperated, that he gets up and punches the kids so hard that he knocks one out and leaves the other one lying in pain.

"What you do to my little brother?" asks the girl as she tries to get up.

"Shut up, puta," says Machete as he gets on top of her again. This time he holds her down by placing his M-16 across her throat. He penetrates her and has one of her nipples in his mouth. As he goes in and out of her, his lust grows murderous. When he reaches his climax, out of utter spite, he bites on her nipple so hard that he bites it off. He spits the raspberry-sized, brown nipple out of his mouth and onto the floor. His mouth and chin drool red with blood.

The girl's eyes become enlarged with agony. At first, she can't scream and rolls in pain holding her breast. She falls off the bed and then lets out ghastly screams, "Ah, Ah, Ah."

"Fuck you. I told you I don't like no gook putas," says Machete pulling up his pants.

"You pay me, you pay me," demands the girl, crying and holding her breast. "You pay me, you pay me," she continues emphatically.

Suddenly Ese walks in, and with subtle restraint says, "We'd better get the fuck out of here cause there's a bunch of pissed-off zipper-heads out in front…they got guns, too. Shit, what's this chick crying about? And what's all that blood doing around your mouth? Oh, you're a nasty fucker. Did you eat this ruca out when she's on the rag?"

"Look what he do to me," says the girl, showing her bleeding breast to Ese.

"Damn, you do hate these gooks, don't you?"

"You pay me," continues the girl pertinaciously.

"Shut the fuck up, whore." Machete tells the girl bringing the M-16 to her head.

"Nel, chale carnal, maliseala.[36] Don't fuck her up or we'll never get out of here alive. Those putos outside are real pissed-off."

"Give me back my sixty," says Machete. They exchange weapons and

---

36. Naw, don't brother, take it easy.

Machete, bristling with rancor, disciplines himself and follows Ese.

Ese leads the way out of the bar. Their inebriation, combat experience and impertinence help them in handling the predicament by not panicking. They thread the M-16 and AK-47 armed mini-mob in a self-defensive and non-threatening posture. Their eyes look halfway toward the crowd and halfway toward the ground. They carry their weapons pointing downward at forty-five degree angles. One hands finger is on the trigger, and the other hand on the barrel guard, ready to pull up and start shooting. They convey the attitude, You might kill us, but we're going to kill some of you, too.

The hostile ad hoc assembly of the National Liberation Front lets them through. They allow Ese and Machete to hop on their jeep and continue on their trek. Speeding away, Ese gives them the finger and shouts, "Chinguen sus madres, pinche putos, and I hope you don't like it." Then, he complains to Machete, "Next time I'm first, carnal."

EPISODE XXII
The Medic

For the second time of his tour of duty, Chuco wakes up in a hospital. He is lying on his stomach when he hears the voice of his friend, Biscuits, saying, "Don't turn over on your back because you may bust open the stitches on your cheeks. Did anybody ever tell you that you have a nice set of buttocks, young man?"

"Quit joking, Biscuits. Is it O.K. if I turn sideways?"

"Try it and see."

Chuco slowly turns on his right side. "That feels better," he tells Biscuits, once he completes the move. "Did any of the guys in my unit get hit?"

"One tall fellow with long sideburns. He died yesterday morning before we left."

That must of been Patillas, thinks Chuco with remorse. Pobre Patillas y su familia.[1] It suddenly occurs to him what Biscuits told him. "Left? Where are we now?" he asks.

"In Da Nang. The hospital in Saigon was full and you and some other patients were flown here to Da Nang. Me and some other medics took care of you guys. Oh, and there was also another one of your buddies that got hit. One with big jack-rabbit ears. He's fine. He got sent back to your unit the next afternoon."

"Ese es la pinche Liebre," [2] says Chuco.

"What?" asks Biscuit.

"That's Jack-Rabbit."

"Why do you guys speak all this Spanish? You from Mexico?"

---

1. "Poor Patillas and his family."
2. "That's fucking Liebre,"

"Some of us, but most of us were born in the U.S. You gringos forget that the Southwest was once Mexico."

Biscuits ignores the subject and continues, "You've been here three days, and the first night, you were delirious with malaria fever. You have malaria, you know. But the fever has broken. You kept talking about someone named Sleepy Eyes. I think you're a good person, so I have requested that you finish recuperating here in Da Nang, so you can help me escort some sick army prisoners back to Saigon when you are well. I figure that will give you some sham time."

"Thanks, Biscuits. I owe you."

"We'll talk about that later. Here comes the nurse to give your quinine."

A nurse, with bright green eyes radiating kindness, approaches Chuco and ask him, "How you feeling, soldier?" She bends over and places a thermometer in Chuco's mouth, her breast wisping his arm.

She smells fresh and clean. He feels a warm heat emitting from her body. Her breasts are voluptuous. He imagines that they are smooth and white like ivory soap. Chuco falls in lust, gets an erection and tells her, "This may sound crazy, m'am, but I've been out in the bush since I've been here in Viet Nam and, well," he stammers, "I was wondering if you could do me a very special favor?"

"Tell me what it is and maybe I can help you," she answers sympathetically.

"I haven't had sex since I've been in Viet Nam, m'am, and I was wondering if I could make love to you."

The nurse's face turns red with anger. How dare this greasy Mexican ask me that, she thinks. Then, she takes a second look at Chuco's sincere expression. "I'm sorry, soldier, but it is against regulations. I suggest you take a cold shower. Here, take this pill and I'll be back tomorrow morning to give you another one," she tells him, handing him a black pill.

Chuco watches her leave and notices the panty lines on her skirt, increasing the demand from his inflamed erection. He doesn't notice that Biscuits has returned until Biscuit says seductively, "Any problems, Chuco?"

"Yeah, I 've got a hard-on that won't quit."

"Maybe I can help," he says, pulling the curtains around Chuco's bed. He grabs some pillows and tells Chuco to turn around on his back, then places them under Chuco's rear end.

Chuco is aware of what is happening, but can't control his sexual agitation. Biscuit first strokes Chuco's penis with his hand, then manipulates it with his mouth. Chuco's open eyes roll back with utmost elation.

Episode XXIII
Heros

On the fourth day of his hospital stay, Chuco is laying on his stomach, bare-assed to air out his wounds, perusing a Playboy magazine. Unexpectedly, someone slaps him on the butt and yells, "¿Q-Vo. De quien chon?"[1]

"Who in the fuck? Quien chingados es, pinche puto," he says grimacing with pain. Then, by the laughter, he can tell it is Ese and Machete.

"Do you remember the last time we saw him? He had two black eyes and a missing tooth," Ese tells Machete.

"That's right. Now somebody's made him a new asshole," answers Machete, laughing hysterically.

"How come he always gets wounded in the ass?"

"Why? Because he's always running away, like a big nalgón,"[2] answers Machete.

"Don't make me laugh. Help me up, vatos, but do it slowly because it hurts if I move too fast." Ese and Machete help Chuco off the bed. Although no one says it, all three are jubilant to be together again.

"Lets get the flock out of here," says Ese.

"I'm not supposed to leave, but I think I can make it," answers Chuco.

"Así me gusta, así son los hombres,"[3] says Machete with a grin.

Ese and Machete anticipated Chuco leaving with them and brought fatigues for him. Chuco takes the fatigues and slowly puts them on.

"Quickly, quickly, maggot. Don't dawdle," says Machete in his drill

1. "What's happening. Who's are they?"
2. booty
3. "That's the way I like it, that's the way men should be,"

sergeant voice.

When Chuco finishes dressing, the three sneak out of the ward. "Let's go to the "steam and cream" I heard all about," says Chuco when they are outside the building. "They say they got some real good putas there. But first, let's go get some pisto."

"Hijo de la chingada. I'm so horny, I'll suck on one of those puta's pussy so hard her tits will cave in. Ain't that right, Machete?" says Ese, winking an eye as a reminder to Machete of the incident with the Vietnamese girl.

"I heard that," he answers. "But let's go get a drink first."

"Chale. Let's go get some panocha first," says Ese.

"Vamos agarrar unos pistos primero.[4] It's two against one Ese. We'll drink a couple of birrias, then we'll go the the 'steam and cream,' " says Chuco.

Machete and Chuco walk to the enlisted men's club because Chuco has a hard time sitting down. Ese drives the jeep to the club and waits for them. When Chuco and Machete reach the club, they walk in together. The air-conditioning makes them feel like they are in paradise. It is the middle of the day and there are only a few soldiers drinking and playing pool. Curtis Mayfield is blasting away on the jukebox.

They walk to the bar, sit down and order three beers. Ese drinks his beer in one gulp and orders another round. "You know what, guys? I've been thinking about staying in the army," says Machete.

"Que!" says Ese in disbelief. You want to be a lifer in this fucking army? I hate this army. Estas baboso."

"Weren't you the one who volunteered for the army and Viet Nam to boot?"

"That's right, but I've changed my mind about this fucking army. I

---

4. "Let's go get the booze first.

can't believe this, Machete. I'll be right back. I've got to go relieve the pressure from my brain," says Ese, walking away and shaking his head.

"What do you think, Chuco?"

"You do what you think is best for you. I just want to get out of the army and go home in one piece."

Three black soldiers walk up to the bar and sit next to Chuco and Machete. "What's happening, brothers?" says one of the soldiers. Flouting military regulations, they wear sunglasses. They also sport black shoelace bracelets and crosses around their necks.

"Nothing much," says Machete.

"How about giving me some dap," says one of the black soldiers extending his hand to Machete.

"I don't do any of that motherfucking handshaking shit," answers Machete disrespectfully.

"Well then, motherfuck you, motherfucker. Motherfucking midget."

"Keep your mama off the streets, motherfucker, then I won't be a motherfucker, motherfucker," answers Machete.

Machete and the soldier attack one another and begin to tussle. A white soldier sees that Chuco and Machete are outnumbered and runs outside to find Ese. He finds him sitting on the latrine holding a hamburger in one hand and a marijuana cigarette in the other. "You the guy with those chingos inside the bar?"

"That's right."

"You'd best get back to the bar, 'cause they done started a fight with some mean and crazy niggers."

Ese throws the hamburger and joint down, cleans himself in a hurry, and rushes to the bar. When he enters the bar, he sees Machete rolling around on the floor with his opponent. Damn, Machete looks like Roy Rogers fighting the bad vatos, thinks Ese. Chuco is holding back the two other soldiers at bay by swinging a cue stick.

Ese bolts to the bar and grabs a whiskey bottle. He surges behind Chuco's adversaries and hits the biggest one on the head with the bottle. To Ese's surprise, the antagonist turns around more furious than before and charges toward him. Ese takes evasive action and runs around the pool table. Ese is too quick for the other soldier, who has blood running down the back of his head, to catch.

The fight is at its height when eight Military Police, blowing whistles, burst in to stop the fight. But this does not deter the soldiers from fighting one another. With billy clubs, the MPs begin to subdue the combatants. The Mexican and black soldiers then begin to fight the MPs instead of one another. However, they are no match for the MPs and their reinforcements. All six soldiers are beaten to the ground and handcuffed, where the MPs continue to beat them until they are unconscious.

The heat is stifling inside the dark connex box. Tiny beams of light infiltrate from the top of the corrugated steel ceiling. Chuco is lying on his left side and like acne, light dots hit the right side of his face. One beam in particular shines directly on his pupil. A thin chain links his handcuffed feet and hands behind his back. He can make out that Ese and Machete are also hog-tied.

"Are you guys awake? Those bastards beat the fuck out of my shoulders," says Machete.

"This time my lip is busted bigger than the last time the marrano[4] in Illusion beat the fuck out of me," laments Chuco.

"Oh, man. I feel bad. Me está llendo hasta la chingada," [5] says Ese, lying on his stomach. Before he can say another word, he pukes a sour and bitter concoction of hamburger meat, recycled beer and stout stomach acid. His retching is so strenuous that he is unable to

---

4. pig
5. I feel like fuck,"

lift his head from the vile stew. When he recovers from the regurgitating fit, he is able to turn to his side and manages to complain, "As Oliver Hardy would say: 'Fine mess you've gotten me into now, Machete.' "

"Get us out of here," yells Machete several times.

Ultimately, an MP walks over to the door, speaks through a square with cut-out metal strips and tells them, "Shut up, spic, or we'll keep you in there for another day."

"Come on, just let us out to take a piss," requests Ese.

"Shut the fuck up. You're lucky we don't go in and beat you again. That guy that looks like a gook broke the jaw of our sergeant major. Good thing the sergeant major is a nigger too, and we don't like him much, or we'd tan your greasy carcasses again for sure."

"He must be talking about you, Machete," says Ese.

"Y'all are some lucky greasers, 'cause your battalion commanders all agreed that it's a better punishment for you to go back to the bush, and that y'all would be of much better use out in the bush than in jail. Them nigger friends of yours ain't gonna be so lucky, 'cause they've done been AWOL and they's going to Long Binh Jail. Thanks for catching them for us."

"They ain't our friends, and we didn't catch nobody for you," rebuts Machete.

"How about me? I'm still recovering from my wounds," says Chuco.

"The doctor says that if you're well enough to go around fighting and drinking, you're well enough to go back to the bush."

Chuco has the best angle to see the MP and notices another person come up to the door, whispering to the MP. "Well I'll be, you sure are some lucky Meskins," says the MP, unlocking the door. He walks into the box and is followed by five other MPs. "Phew! you're some smelly sons-a-bitches," grumbles the MP.

When their cuffs are removed, the prisoners stiffly get up and creak out the door. Ese reeks of puke. Up-chucked hamburger meat is glued to his shirt. The back of his head is crusted with dried blood. Chuco's cheeks are purple and black; his eyes and lips distended. Machete walks out like a rickety old man, one shoulder sloped and limping, his pants wet from piss.

Episode XXIV
Soldier Without A Soul

Chuco feels someone tapping his shoulder and yelling at him, "Get up soldier, you're home."

"I'm home, that can't be," he whispers. For an instant, he forgets the noise of the helicopter and that he is in Viet Nam. He gathers himself and his gear and jumps off the helicopter. His eyes are swollen and can barely make out his company headquarters building. He enters headquarters as a Sergeant E-5 and, like Ese and Machete at their unit headquarters, leaves the building a Private First-Class E-3.

His orders are to report to the helicopter landing pad immediately. On the way to the pad, he stops at the mess hall. Chuco peers through a wire screen and shouts inside at his friend the cook. "Órale, ¿Comal, que pasa?"

"¿Q-vo cuñado," says the cook with a round, Olmec face.

"¿A dónde has estado?" [1]

"I was taking my R&R. Y ya me voy para el bush. ¿Me puedes hacer unos tacos de volada?"

"Sirol, cuñado, como que no. Pasale por la back door. Y de volada te hago unos tacos de carne." [2] Besides his genuine congeniality, Comal's willingness to cook Mexican food, especially flour tortillas, make him a most popular trooper among the Chicano soldiers

"Hijo de la chinelas. ¿Qué te pasó a ti?" [3] says Comal when Chuco

---

1. "What's happening Comal?
   "What's up brother in law
   "Where have you been?"
2. I'm leaving for the bush. Can you make me some quick tacos."
   "Sure brother in law. Come through the back door and I'll make
   you some meat tacos."
3. "Son of a gun. What happened to you?"

walks in. "Sit down," he says, handing Chuco a beer.

"Me and my camaradas got in a fight con unos mayates,[4] and then the juras[5] beat the shit out of all of us. They let us out of jail to come back to the bush."

"Se me hace que[6] it would have been better for you if you would have stayed in the bote.[7] Because a vido un chingo de chingazos.[8] Did you know that Bravo company got wiped out?" asks Comal as he turns the tortillas on the grill. "They've brought in un frego de[9] new guys in as replacements."

"Can you make those tacos to go, cuñado? I think I hear the shithook helicopters coming," says Chuco.

"Sirol, cuñado." answers Comal, wrapping the flour tacos in a cloth napkin. "Andale, aquí está una birronga más," [10] he says, handing Chuco another beer.

Chuco takes the beer and hurries to the helicopter landing pad. When he gets there, he is stunned when he sees a hundred or so new recruits waiting to board two Chinooks. Chuco is the last to enter his helicopter. The interior of the Chinook would have seemed to Jonah that he was inside a large metal whale, muses Chuco.

Once Chuco settles in, he takes out his bundle of tacos and nibbles gingerly on one of them from the side of his mouth. He sees a hodge-podge of "cherries," as new guys are referred to, in varying heights, weights and colors, but all absolutely young. He recognizes, with marked consternation, their grim innocence. Fear and steel helmets weigh down the soldiers' heads towards the metal floor. The ubiqui-

---

4. with some blacks,
5. police
6. "I think
7. can
8. there's been plenty of fighting.
9. a lot of
10. "Here, take another brew,"

tous, black, Matty Mattel M-16 rifles are held between the soldiers' legs with the barrels pointed down.

The new soldiers remind Chuco of the time when he arrived in Viet Nam. Then it dawns on him why the singing, drunk soldier was yelling at them when they got off the plane, "You're all going to die." That little vato did it because he wanted to sober us up and to face the fact that some of us are going to die in Viet Nam. He was telling us that if we fight hard enough we can survive, like he did, he thinks.

In a quixotic fit, Chuco gets up from his seat and starts yelling, "All right, all you motherfuckers, if there's a hell below, you're all gonna go. You're all going to die over here in Nam." He says this over and over as he walks up and down the aisle to make sure all the soldiers can hear him above the resounding chatter of the helicopter blades. Most of the soldiers pretend they don't hear him. Occasionally, a soldier will respond by lifting his head in obligatory bewilderment.

When they touch ground, the soldiers in Chuco's helicopter have put aside their fears and are relieved they don't have to hear what seems to them unpleasant, daft blustering. Chuco is the first one out of the helicopter. He stands between the two files of off-loading, and gives commands in Spanish as they run out of the helicopter.

"Órale, todos los Chicanos ponganse aca para un lado."[11] He scrutinizes the soldiers to make sure no Chicanos pass by him.

Seven soldiers stand to the side waiting for further orders from Chuco. The second to the last soldier that runs by is grabbed by Chuco and is told, "Can't you understand Spanish?"

"No," responds the soldier."

"Where you from?" asks Chuco.

"I'm from Michigan."

"You're a fucking Mexican, aren't you?"

---

11. "All right all the Chicanos come line up to the side."

"Sure."

"Then get in line." He looks over the eight soldiers, "¿Y tú, a poco eres mexicano?" [12] He asks one of the soldiers with what he considers prominent African features.

"No, pero hablo español." [13]

"You're O.K., then," says Chuco. "You guys wait here. I'll go look for our company area." All around the landing are soldiers moving ammunition, supplies and artillery pieces. Combat engineers have been brought in to fortify the perimeter. In the distance, jets and cobra helicopters swoop in on their targets with bombs and rockets.

This is a big operation, surmises Chuco, as he finally locates his company headquarters. The command post is a small area of levelled elephant grass. "I need to know where my platoon is at," he says to the company commander's radioman.

"You'll have to wait," he is told, "until the captain finishes talking with Charlie company's captain." The radioman is so busy directing artillery fire that he forgets Chuco is next to him. A few feet away, behind some tall elephant grass, Chuco can hear the company commander talking to Charlie company's captain.

"Don't worry, captain, I've already sent my Mexican platoon to lead the way of the offensive."

"Do you think that is prudent at this point? Shouldn't you lay more artillery in that area to soften up the enemy? Intelligence tells us that the enemy is very well dug in there," says the Charlie Company commander.

"We have to clear that area now so we can catch the gooks between us and the 23rd Battalion and cream those commie bastards," says the captain with a heinous smirk on his face. "Sometimes we have to take

---

12. "And you, I suppose your a Mexican?"
13. "No, but I speak Spanish,"

chances we don't like to take, captain."

Hijo de la chingada. I'd better get Ro-Ro and the vatos or else they're going to get fucked up bad. The captain is sending them straight into an ambush, thinks Chuco. "Where's my platoon?" he asks the radioman urgently.

"Can't you see I'm talking on the radio?"

"Listen, motherfucker, you'd better tell me now or I'm going to blow your fucking head off," Chuco tells him with his M-16 at the radioman's head.

"Hell, man. Don't get excited," says the radioman, showing him on the map where the platoon is at.

"All right now, get them on the horn so I can talk to them," orders Chuco, lowering his M-16.

The radioman tries to call the platoon but can't contact them. Chuco runs back to where the new guys are at and tells them to leave their packs and carry all the ammunition and grenades they can. Chuco and his ragtail squad hurry to catch Ro-Ro and the platoon before they run into the ambush.

For two kilometers, Chuco leads his squad through heavy marsh and swamp. The new soldiers are not used to this type of stressful, physical and mental vigor. Two weeks earlier, they had been home on leave in a whole different world. Most of them had been high school students six months earlier. He pushes them to the point of near collapse.

When they reach the platoon, they have already fallen into an ambush. Chuco assesses the situation. He can see Ro-Ro and Liebre pinned down by Viet Congs in one-man spider holes. Several soldiers lie dead and many more are wounded. If he doesn't take action quickly, all his platoon will be killed. He figures that the only way to save the platoon is by going around the enemy and catching them from behind.

Chuco knows that when Ro-Ro sees him attacking the enemy from the rear he will also advance against their foes. Chuco leads his squad around and behind the enemy. Heavy foliage makes it difficult to shoot at the enemy from a distance, so Chuco and his squad get close to the unsuspecting enemy.

As Chuco's squad opens fire, he begins to yell at Ro-Ro, "Aquí estamos,[14] Ro-Ro, get your ass up." The fire fight that ensues is vicious. The fighting takes place at very close quarters. Chuco perceives the fire fight as a surrealistic, two-dimensional event in slow motion. Time, space and reality are no longer what they seem, or pretend to be. Like busted balloons, people's heads are shattered. Teeth, ears, and other small body parts fall to the ground like bones and wasted meat on a butcher's floor.

When the fire fight slackens, the dead and the living converge in communion. The encounter is so intense that Chuco's soul leaves with the souls of the dead. Chuco doesn't feel his soul depart because his shocked mind and body waver between the reality of death and pretensions of life.

After the fire fight is over, Chicano and Vietnamese bodies are strewn like a jig-saw puzzle with their blood mixing in the earth. Chuco sees Ro-Ro kneeling and praying in grief over the lifeless body of Liebre. Helicopters are called in to evacuate the wounded. After the wounded are placed on the helicopters, the expired are loaded on helicopters for the first leg of their final journey home.

All of Chuco's ragtail squad of new guys have been killed. I didn't even know their names, he reflects. An eerie feeling overcomes him when he helps stack the unknown soldiers up on one another like sides of beef. The bodies are not even put in body bags. Like tears from heaven, a light rain falls as the helicopters take off. With their

14. "We're here,

hair blowing freely, the eyes of the dead stare blankly toward the sky. They seem to know that they are dead.

For the next four days, the fighting continues. Out of sheer exhaustion both the Viet Cong and U.S. Army back off from one another. Chuco's platoon is down to twelve men. The captain was slightly wounded and evacuated during the operation. He is waiting for the company when they return to their base camp.

Chuco feels something is missing but can't figure it out. Even Ro-Ro tells him, "¿Que te pasa? No te vez igual."

"I don't know, pero si me siento diferente." [15]

When they reach their base camp, some of the other Chicanos from other platoons come over with beer, marijuana and liquor. Guitars are brought out and music is played. Chuco feels that it is the right time to tell Ro-Ro that the captain sent them into an ambush on purpose. "Fíjate, Ro-Ro, que el pinche capitan, Mr. Charley, te mando en un ambush on purpose. It was that day cuando llege yo. ¿Te acuerdas?"

"¿Que?"

"Sí," answers Chuco. "Le tenemos que dar en la madre."

"Como qué no. Le tenemos qué dar en la torre."

"Ponganse truchas, calabazas," [16] announces Chuco. The guitars stop playing and the soldiers listen attentively. "The captain sent our platoon on an ambush on purpose. He's done that to the negros a couple of times before. Y es tiempo que [17] somebody kills him before he kills more of us."

---

15. "What happening to you, you don't look the same."
   but I feel different."
16. "Check this out Ro-Ro, the fucking captain Mr. Charlie sent you on an ambush on purpose. It was that day I showed up. Do you remember?"
   "What?"
   "Yes, answers Chuco. "We have to kill him."
   "Pay attention dummies,"
17. "It's high time"

"Como dicia, la Liebre, 'sirol.' Yo le doy en la madre," says Ro-Ro.

"Yo tengo mejor idea.[18] Let's put all our money together. Y el que lo mata,[19] gets all the money," says Chuco.

"Buena idea," says one soldier, as all of the soldiers agree with Chuco's proposal. Chuco takes off his bush hat and passes it around. All the soldiers put money in the hat and when it gets back to Chuco, he counts two hundred and three dollars of military payment certificates, "funny money," as the soldiers call it.

"Remember, whoever kills the captain gets all the feria," says Chuco, raising his beer as a gesture of approval.

All the soldiers hold their cans or bottles up in the air, yelling in solidarity, "Muerte. Muerte. Para el capitan."

"Que siga la pachanga," [20] says Ro-Ro, picking up a guitar and begins to play a Mexican Revolutionary song, "Soy Soldado de Pancho Villa."The setting sun contrives silhouettes of the soldiers as if they are actually soldiers of Pancho Villa.

After a few more songs, Ro-Ro sings his favorite song, "Mi Ultima Parranda." He strums the guitar and sings with melancholy. Brusquely, in the middle of the song, the captain appears and begins to upbraid the soldiers. "You Goddamn Mexicans think you can do anything you want. Drinking and smoking marijuana on the perimeter is against regulations. I'm going to make sure you all get court-martialed."

Without a second thought, Ro-Ro picks up his M-16 and unloads a full magazine of bullets into the captain's chest. The captain briefly realizes what has happened and falls dead. Two soldiers pick the captain up and throw him over the trench. Cholo gets up on the trench

---

18. "Like Liebre used to say, 'sure' I'll kill him,"
   "I've got a better idea.
19. And the one who kills him
20. "Death. Death. For the captain
   "Let the party continue"

and peppers the captain with a few rounds of his M-60 machine gun to make sure he is dead.

Chuco walks over to Ro-Ro and hands him the bounty money. Ro-Ro takes it and throws it in the air and says, "Yo no mato por dinero. Lo mate porque no lo quieria."[21] He takes a deep drink of tequila and continues to sing and play the guitar.

Chuco calls on the radio, "Alpha 3, 4. This is Bravo 8, 9, the captain has been shot and killed by enemy snipers."

---

21. "I don't kill for money. I killed him because I didn't like him."

EPISODE XXV
Rats and Chile Beans

The monsoon has begun. It rains and rains for hours, days and weeks at a time. The deluge makes the soldiers miserable. They are hostages to rain. The moisture makes their skins peel off and some of them get jungle rot on their crotches. Leeches, two inch blood-suckers, come out in droves and live off of the soldiers. It has been raining incessantly for five days, and the food has run out.

The company has set up a perimeter next to an angry and swollen river. It's late afternoon, and Ese is in a foxhole with Three Bears.

"Man, I'm getting hungry. It's been two days since we've had anything to eat. I could sure go for some of my mom's enchiladas, refried beans and rice. She takes corn tortillas, rolls and fries them with white Monterrey Jack cheese, or sometimes she'll make them with yellow-orange Longhorn cheese. She puts onions and olives in between, topped with fresh green lettuce and tomatoes. On top of that, more black olives and raw onions thrown in for good measure. The red chile sauce she makes from scratch. She uses these long, red, New Mexico dried chilies and puts them in a hand grinder. I don't care how fancy other people cook, like the French or Italians, but my jefita's refried beans are some of the best food in the world.

"I didn't know how good I had it. Can you imagine, I used to complain that I didn't like too much tomato sauce or onions in the rice. I swear to God when I get home I'll never complain again."

"Sometimes after the track meets, some of us would have enough money to go to the Jolly Kone and buy some monster burgers. Man, are they good. The french fries are also real good. Nice and brown on the outside and soft inside. They would be so hot that the warm air would steam out of them when you bit them. I liked to eat them with a lot of thick, thick ketchup. The fries go real good with a monster cherry coke with plenty of ice."

"Be quiet, Knucklehead. Quit talking about food, it only makes it worse," says Three Bears.

"It looks like spit is coming out of your mouth there, my man," laughs Ese, noticing that Three Bears is drooling. So he continues, just to be mean. "When I was a little kid, we used to pick cotton and my father used to make hamburgers and chile beans and sell them in the cotton fields from a teeny trailer. Now those were some good hamburgers. Oh!, and the chile beans were even better. Is that a puto oso growl I hear or what?"

"You're so fucking funny, Knucklehead. I almost forgot to laugh. You know that's my stomach. Wait! Do you see what I see?" says Three Bears, pointing to a rice paddy in front of them.

"Dinks?" Ese says as he takes the safety off his M-16.

"No, stupid! Rats."

"Oh yeah, I see them. I hate those fuckers. What about them?" asks Ese.

"Get some of the other guys to help us catch some of those rats so we can eat them," says Three Bears with bulging eyes.

"What! I ain't going to eat no dirty rats."

"Quit your bullshitting and go and get Shorty and his squad," orders Three Bears.

Ese returns with Shorty and his squad. Word has been given down the line that a squad is moving a few yards up from the perimeter. This is very dangerous because sometimes not everyone gets the word or someone panics, usually a new guy, and the squad can be shot by their own men. Many of the soldiers are not sure if they want to eat rat, but their hunger begins to prevail over their cultural biases, so they move out. Two men stay on guard while the rest beat the rats to death with their steel pots. Ese is squeamish about picking up the rats, but does so nonetheless.

"Don't be such a snagglepuss," laughs Three Bears.

Ese has been terrified of rats ever since he was ten. One night when they were living in a barn, he and his brother were sleeping on the floor and a rat ran across his chest and face and scared the holy shit out of him. He still shudders at the memory of the rat's baleful screech and tiny human-like feet running across his face.

The soldiers manage to kill ten rats. Most of the rats have their heads smashed in. They are fat and healthy, just right for eating. The rats' feet are tied together with wire and carried to the perimeter. Three Bears orders the construction of a lean-to. It doesn't take more than three minutes before Ese and Bones make one.

In the meantime, Shorty and Three Bears begin to skin the rats. They lay the heads on a piece of wood and chop them off. Both of them are country boys, so killing and skinning animals is something they are experienced at. After the heads and intestines are removed, they peel the skins off with surgical dexterity.

"Hot digidy-dog, we got ourselves some baby rabbit here," says Three Bears with glee as he holds up the red fleshed rats in the rain to wash. "You guys ready with the sticks?" he asks.

"Here they are," says Ese as he hands them to Three Bears.

Three Bears and Shorty fit the rats on skewers. Ese has built a small fire made of grass, leaves, twigs and heat tabs. The meat is held over the fire and rotated frequently. The men gather around underneath the lean-to, staring at the cooking meat like depraved vultures.

"Man, just look at this meat, it's what your people call carne asada, ain't it, Knucklehead?" teases Three Bears.

"Shit, here comes our man in Viet Nam, Captain America and his suck-ass lieutenant" says Ese in his customary irreverence for authority. It isn't that he naturally dislikes authority, but he is repugnant toward individuals who use their personal weaknesses to abuse it. This, to him, is the general rule.

"Sergeant Three Bears, what is going on here? What are you men doing lighting a fire and leaving the perimeter without permission?" asks the captain, a tall blond, West Point graduate, with his muscular lieutenant, an ex-Michigan State football player, at his side.

"We're just cooking rat meat we caught outside the perimeter, sir," answers Three Bears in a diplomatic, yet unintimidated voice. "You see how good this meat is cooking?" says Three Bears as he turns the meat. "See how brown it's turning? It'll be done in a couple of minutes," he titillates. The captain and his lieutenant gawk at the meat with carnivorous lasciviousness.

"Here, Captain, you take the first piece," says Three Bears, putting a skewered rat to his face.

A succulent aroma of cooked meat travels up his nostrils. The captain is hesitant to take the meat because he was about to upbraid the men for going outside the perimeter and killing the rats; and because he is an officer. The captain is in indecisive agony as his stomach grumbles.

Ese senses this, so to defy the captain and show him he has more balls than he, Ese takes his rat to his mouth and gives it a big bite. He closes his eyes in gastronomical ecstasy. Before he can take another bite, the others follow suit and devour the meat like voracious piranhas.

After the feast, the captain orders the lieutenant, "Give the word to all the platoon leaders to send out a squad of men each and hunt rats."

Ese thinks to himself, "This vato acts as if it was his idea to kill the rats."

As the captain leaves, he tells Three Bears, "Sergeant, I have one month left in the bush. When I leave, I'm going to take your squad with me to the rear."

The soldiers react, except for Three Bears, with an astonished relief of reprieved, condemned men. If they can survive for one more month, it is an almost sure thing that they will leave Viet Nam alive and in one piece.

Ese and Three Bears go back to their foxhole. The deluge continues to make them miserable.

"Did you hear what Captain Puto said? When he leaves the bush, he's going to take us with him to a sham job in the rear; then we won't have to hump the bush. We'll be living the life of fat rats. We can sleep in a nice clean bed every night. We can eat hot food," says Ese with rapture.

"I'd rather do my time out here because the officers and lifers will harass us all the time. You're such a fuck-up that you'll be in trouble all of the time. And anyway, we'll get fat."

"We can drink all the beer we want," says Ese.

"We'll probably turn into alcoholics," answers Three Bears.

"We can fuck the hootch maids."

"We'll probably get the fatal "your-weenie-falls-off-syphilis" and be sent to that island in the Pacific Ocean where they send all those GIs to die."

"We can smoke all the dew we can do."

"We'll probably get busted and go to Long Binh Jail for smoking that shit."

"Hijola, you can fuck up a wet dream," complains Ese.

"Pipe down and let me get some sleep, you stupid knucklehead."

"Oso-Bears."

"What now?" he snarls. "I'm trying to get some sleep."

"I can't wait to get back home so I can be like Cadillac says, 'Laying in the cut. Bigger than shit, bigger than do-do.' If I ever get another chance to get back to the rear, this time for sure I'm going to go to one of those 'steam and cream' places. What do you like the best on a girl, her tits, her ass, or maybe her mug?"

"Shut the fuck up."

"Come on, Oso, don't be like that, carnal. Tell me. O.K.?"

Three Bears places his hand on his forehead and slowly rubs his face down and hesitantly says, "I like a woman's ears."

"What!" exclaims Ese. "Oso. That's the dumbest thing I ever heard of. Or as Bullwinkle would say, 'That's the most unheard of thing I ever heard of.' An ear? With all that wax!"

"No, stupid." Three Bears demonstrates with his right hand. "It's the way it curves, her ear reaching from the middle of her head to where it's even to her mouth; then I can French kiss that orifice. Her lobe is like her clit, just kind of smooth and just like…nudely unexposed, just hanging there."

"What if she doesn't have big hanging lobes?"

"Then I don't like her because that means she has a little clit."

"Man, that sure is dumb."

"Oh, yeah. What do you look for in a woman?"

"I like toes and underarms."

"Fuck, you're sick. I don't want to hear it. Let me get some fucking shut-eye. Wake me up when it's my turn for guard."

"No te aguites mi Osito. Oso?" [1]

"What?" he snarls again.

"What's your favorite dish? Do you guys really eat buffalos and acorns, and live in tepees over there in South Dakota?"

Three Bears shakes his head in disbelief and falls into a shallow

---

1. "Don't get mad my little bear. Bear?"

sleep.

The end of a miserable rainy night introduces a miserable rainy morning.

Three Bears nudges Ese and tells him, "Wake up, Knucklehead, it's time to move out."

Ese wakes up, faking disbelief, he says, "I'm still here. Man, I'm hornier than a double-lipped dog. I've got so much cheese in my chest, I think I'm going to bust. Right now, I'd fuck a pile of rocks if I thought there was a snake in it. The crack of dawn ain't even safe around me."

"Shut up stupid. Our platoon is walking the point and you're the pointman."

As happy-go-lucky as Ese acts, his skills and acumen at being the first man to lead the company are outstanding. He has an uncanny sense of vision, hearing and even smell; and his ability to feel the presence of spirits is unearthly.

Ese lights a cigarette under his poncho, takes deep drags off it and questions for the first time, What am I doing here?

"Let's go, Knucklehead, move out. We're going to walk along the river for a few klicks and wait to be re-supplied. The captain has promised us we're going to get mail," says Three Bears.

"All right, all right," answers Ese.

The company moves up alongside the river for a couple of hours before they stop. Then the order is given that they should go back in the same direction that they came from. The soldiers grumble and complain like all infantrymen have for hundreds of years. And as usual, they comply nonetheless.

When they reach their previous night-lodger, Ese passes down a warning to the men behind him not to touch anything laying on the ground, because it might be booby-trapped. After Ese has lost sight of the night-lodger, he hears an explosion. He thinks, I told the stupid motherfuckers. Don't they understand that we're always being followed?

They wait for the rest of the company to catch up, and he hears over the prick twenty-five radio that one soldier has been killed and two wounded. Stupid motherfuckers, babosos, he thinks again.

The rain continues its ruthless punishment. The company finally reaches its destination. They set up a perimeter in their usual, efficient manner. Everyone ignores the dead soldier in a body bag, as if trying to deny that death exists. Because the wounded will be sent to a dry hospital, or maybe even home, they are looked on with envy by the rest of the soldiers. After an hour, the rain incredulously slackens and the familiar, sporadic thumping sound of Huey helicopters is heard.

Three of the four helicopters are able to land. They off-load ammunition and C-rations. The dead soldier and wounded are loaded before the rain begins to fall in even greater ferocity than before. The fourth helicopter, loaded with mail, is unable to land, so the crew throws a red plastic bag full of mail from a hundred feet off the ground. The soldiers become animated at the idea of mail. If there is anything that works wonders for the morale of soldiers, it is mail.

They wait with great anticipation as the bag is thrown out of the helicopter. Like jilted lovers, they watch it fall in the river.

Without hesitation, Shorty, from Ese's platoon, jumps in the river. To the amazement of the soldiers, he is able to retrieve the bag. He brings it ashore to the captain who tells him, "Outstanding, young man. Tarzan couldn't have done better." A couple of soldiers pat him on the back, as if he had just scored a touchdown.

In typical military organizational fashion, everything is broken from structurally larger units to smaller ones. The mail is first sorted by platoon. From platoon, it is broken down by squad. Eventually, everyone gets their mail, except for Shorty. Everyone is too busy reading their mail under their ponchos to notice Shorty sitting on his steel pot, oblivious to the rain.

"Next time I'm in the rear, it's for sure I'll make it to one of those 'steam and cream' places that I've heard so much about. You know, those steam baths that have those puta mamasotas. Last time, I almost made it, but that crazy Machete had to start some shit."

"You're as full of shit as a Christmas turkey," retorts Three Bears under his poncho, "You'd better watch out for those chicks because they sometimes put razor blades up and in their pussies."

"I don't give a flying-fuck, it's worth it...just to get laid. I can't wait," he concludes as he takes off the poncho over his head. The first thing he notices is Shorty sitting on his steel pot. "What happened, carnal, didn't you get any mail?"

"No, nadien me ha escrito en cuatro meses,"[2] says Shorty.

"Four months, man, doesn't anybody know how to write in your family?"

"Sí," answers Shorty sadly.

"Man, if you haven't received anything by now, I'd forget about it. Here, read some of my mail."

"No gracias."[3]

"Hijo, I'm glad I'm not in your family. Estan hasta la chingada,"[4] says Ese with delayed regret.

"Chingo-San," he hears a voice behind him call out. Immediately he knows it's Beaucoup, the South Vietnamese translator, because he is the only one that calls him this. He is called Beaucoup because of his repeated use of the word beaucoup.

"Well, I'll be. If it ain't my cuñado, Beaucoup. How was your leave?

---

2. "No, no one has written to me in four months,"

3. "No thanks."

4. They are all messed up,"

"Very, very beaucoup," he says in his Vietnamese accent. "Here, I have the batteries for your radio that you asked for," he says, as he hands them to Ese.

"Thanks, carnal," says Ese with gratitude. "Now I can listen to some music at night." For the soldiers who are lucky enough to obtain transistor radio batteries, they can put on ear plugs to listen to the radio; if they are fortunate enough to receive a station.

"My wife have baby boy, now I have two daughters and a son. In one more month, I am going to be re-assigned to Saigon and I will be with them again."

"That's great."

Three Bears walks up to them, and Beaucoup shakes Three Bear's hand and tells him, "It's good to see you, Mr. Sergeant Three Bears."

"It's good to see you, too. Sorry to break up the party, but we've got to hump into the Iron Triangle and meet with the rest of the battalion," says Three Bears with apprehension.

Beaucoup's happy face quickly turns serious. "That's not good. Beaucoup VC, beaucoup VC there," he repeats, as is the tendency of people who aren't fluent in a foreign language. "The Japanese and the French lose some terrible battles there. They have dug many, many kilometers of tunnels for the past twenty-five years. At night, they say that the spirits of the dead soldiers fight the battles again. It is not good to go there."

"Well, we don't have much of a choice. Gear up and let's get moving," says Three Bears.

As usual, the soldiers moan and groan, but move out nonetheless. The rain keeps pounding.

They walk until it is almost nightfall. When they stop for the night, everyone immediately digs in. They follow their standard operating procedure of placing claymore mines and trip flares around the perimeter. Everyone is assigned their turn for guard. The captain calls in their position to headquarters Three Bears and Ese get as comfortable as possible in their foxhole. Three Bears has the first guard and Ese is so exhausted, he goes to sleep without talking or even thinking about the rain.

In the middle of the night, Three Bears taps Ese on the shoulder to wake him for his turn on guard. Ese rubs his face and is relieved that the rain has stopped. Seven days, he thinks, siete dias it's been raining without stopping, until now.

A full moon glows in the middle of an abandoned French Michelan rubber plantation. Jungle plants have reasserted their natural growing rights. They seem like the Vietnamese who have begun to reclaim their traditional territory. The rays of the moon induce the wet leaves to sparkle like translucent star clusters in a faraway galaxy.

Plop, plop, sound the drops of water as they hit the leaves on the ground. Is that a Viet Cong or is it just the rain? questions Ese. He stares to the front of him and can't decide if it's the sound of human movement or water drops. Naw, nomás son las[5] drops, he decides.

Moments later, he thinks he sees mists of water forming into obscure human configurations. Naw that's bullshit, he reasons. An instant later he sees the same thing. Hijo de su pinche madre. This is bullshit. I don't feel anybody that close.

He nudges Three Bears and warns him, "Psst, psst, hey, get up. I think I see movement out in front," whispers Ese.

Three Bears promptly becomes alert, "Where?"

"I'm not sure if it's anything, but up front."

Three Bears has great confidence in Ese's combat senses and stays awake.

"Do you still have that reefer in your wallet?" asks Three Bears.

5. "Naw, it's only

"You know I do. It's in the plastic baggie with Chanclas' hairs."

"Well, bring it out and light it under your poncho and give me a drag after you're done."

"Sure, boss."

Ese goes under his poncho in order to not allow the light of the match and marijuana cigarette to give them away. He emerges with a happy face and gives the cigarette to Three Bears.

"Do you see what I see?" asks Ese

"Is it vapor spirits?" ask Three Bears.

"Yep."

Ese and Three Bears find it hard to believe the diaphanous apparitions of French and Vietnamese soldiers fighting hand to hand with one another. The engagement is fierce; magnificent lurid colors take the place of sound. Clashing bayonets generate savage hues of hate. French eyes emitting vehement amber rays are countered by Vietnamese glowerings of scintillating red, creating an orange landscape. The mortally wounded fall, dissipating into the ground. Eventually, the French are defeated, and the evanescent Vietnamese bid farewell with their rifles to Ese and Three Bears.

"Man, that's some dynamite weed," says Three Bears in disbelief.

They are shocked, but not terrified, of what they have just seen. It is living people, not spirits, they are afraid of.

"Don't tell nobody, Three Bears, because ain't nobody going to believe us."

"I heard that," agrees Three Bears.

They both stay up until daybreak and act as if nothing happened the previous night. Three Bears reports to the lieutenant, whom everyone calls LT. He is a thin, red-headed Jewish fellow from New York City with a personality semblance to Woody Allen. The lieutenant receives orders from the company commander and gives them to Three Bears, who makes sure they are carried out. However, Three Bears, for the most part, is the defacto leader of the platoon.

After the briefing, Three Bears returns to the platoon and tells them, "We are walking drag. It's a good thing, too, because we are going into the heart of the Iron Triangle to meet up with the rest of the battalion."

"Three Bears, does that mean we have to dress up like girls?"

"Your so fucking funny Knucklehead," says Three Bears, holding back his laughter.

The rain continues. The company walks for several hours before they finally meet with the battalion. Quickly, ersatz bunkers are constructed in a circle, twenty meters from one another. On the morning of the second day of the operation, Bravo, Charlie and Delta companies move out with the objective to search and destroy the enemy. Alpha company stays behind to guard the base camp.

There is no contact with the enemy, and the battalion returns to the base camp at dusk. The following morning, Ese's company stays behind to guard the base camp. The rest of the battalion moves out again using the same path as the previous day. Once again, there is no contact and the battalion returns to the base camp earlier than before.

Ese and Three Bears are busy making sure all the defensive arrangements are complete. Ese turns to his left and notices Beaucoup motioning to him in the traditional Vietnamese hand signal, palms face down and waving the fingers up and down. To the soldiers, it resembles a good-bye, but Ese is familiar with this motion because it is also similar to the way Mexicans motion to call people.

Ese walks to Beaucoup and asks him, "What's the scoop Beaucoup?"

"Are we going to move out again tomorrow using the same path we did today and yesterday?

"From what I understand, yeah."

"No, we cannot do that. It is too dangerous," says Beaucoup with the thought of death chilling him. "Remember, this is the Iron Triangle, there are tunnel complexes everywhere. The communists can come out of anywhere. They will be dug in and waiting for us," he exhorts.

"Naw, I don't think they can ambush three hundred men," says Ese with skepticism.

"No, Chingo-san. I have been fighting the communists for five years and I know how they work. Also Cookie, the Kit Carson scout, used to be a VC and he thinks the same thing."

"Well, I don't trust that vato. He used to be a VC and for me he's a traitor. What's to keep him from being a traitor again. Once a traitor, always a traitor, as far as I'm concerned."

"Yes, I agree with you. I do not trust him either, but he does not want to die. He will be walking with your point platoon."

Ese is silent for a moment and seriously contemplates what Beaucoup has told him. "Let's go and talk to Three Bears and see what he thinks," suggests Ese.

They walk a couple of hundred feet to where Three Bears is busy reinforcing a bunker.

"Hey, Three Bears, I think we got some problems," says Ese.

"What kind of problems, other than we're Indians in Viet Nam," he says with a grin.

"No, I'm serious."

"Shit, you haven't been serious since the Liberty Bell cracked."

"You tell him, Beaucoup. He won't listen to me," says Ese as he shakes his head.

Beaucoup retells what he told Ese. After Beaucoup explains, Three Bears gently bites his lower lip and nods, "I think you've got a good point. I've heard about them tunnels. They are deadly. It is dumb to take the same trail three times in a row anyway," says Three Bears with apprehension. "You wait here, Knucklehead, me and Beaucoup will go talk to the LT."

Reaching their lieutenant's position, Beaucoup once again explains his projection. The lieutenant is somewhat convinced and asks, "What do you want to do about it? I don't have anything to say about things like this."

"Go tell the captain so he can tell the battalion commander. You know the chain of command, LT," says Three Bears.

"I don't think that's a good idea." says the lieutenant.

"Goddammit, LT. Have a fucking pair. It's our turn to walk the point tomorrow, and I'll be fucked if I'm going into an ambush if I can help it. In fact, we could fuck them up. All we have to do is act as if we're going out in full strength the same way we have the last couple of days, and send out a company as a decoy. Then we send two other companies about fifty meters to the left and right flanks; we'll come right up behind them if there is an ambush, then we can catch them in a crossfire. Shit, anything is better than running into an ambush."

"It sounds plausible, but I don't think the captain will listen to me."

Three Bears' face becomes flushed with anger as he grits his teeth. He tells the lieutenant as he leaves in a huff, "You're about as worthless as tits on a boar hog, LT."

Returning to the bunker, Beacucoup, Ese, and Three Bears discuss what they can do about their situation.

"I would sure hate to turn into one of those spirit soldiers we seen last night," says Ese with subdued terror.

Beaucoup smiles and says, "I saw them, too."

"We've got to talk to the other men and see what they think. You stay here, Beacucoup, and me and Ese will go around to the other bunkers and talk to the sergeants and see what they think," says

Three Bears.

Night has arrived, and wondrously, the rain has stopped. Three Bears and Ese maneuver their way around the perimeter. They talk to the people in their own platoon and company first. All of Three Bears' squad agrees with him and Ese. From there, they work their way around to the three other companies, talking to the men. Though not all the soldiers they speak to know them personally, many are familiar with Ese's and Three Bears' reputations and exploits.

Most of the arguments given by the soldiers are similar. "We've got to do our duty." To this, Ese and Three Bears reply, "That's true, but you've got to be alive to do that; if we take the same route again, we ain't going to be alive." Another reason given is, "I've only got a short time to go and I don't want to go to prison." To this, Ese and Three Bears answer, "If we all stick together, they can't send us all to jail. Besides, if we don't stick together, you won't have to worry about going to jail or going back to the world, except in a body bag."

A majority of the soldiers agree that it is a dangerous move, but are doubtful about not following orders. They know of the serious repercussions if they refuse to move out in the morning. The military has done an excellent job in training these soldiers to obey orders. But Ese and Three Bears have nonetheless convinced more than a few soldiers.

In the pre-dawn hours, Three Bears and Ese make their way back to their bunker. Ese gazes at the last remaining stars and becomes homesick. He remembers when he and Muñeca used to walk next to the cotton fields, holding hands and looking up at the stars. That reality seems as if it never existed. The stars now seem closer than Illusion because at least the stars are close enough to see.

Morning arrives quickly, and the order is given to move out. As the battalion prepares to move, Ese, Da-Da, Cadillac and Three Bears, make one last desperate attempt to convince the soldiers not to move out. The relative security of daylight and the well-fortified perimeter allow for a few soldiers to cluster. They take sides: "I ain't going in there. You guys are sick from your motherfucking asses if you think I'm going in there," says Ese.

"Bullshit, you ain't nothing but a chicken-shit Mexican," says Hollywood, a former highway policeman.

"Go suck your mama's ass, you punk-redneck-puto," says Ese holding his M-16, ready to bring it up and fire. "Lots of you guys know that I've always walked the point and I've never backed down from the dinks. But I ain't going to walk into an ambush. I just ain't. I'll lead you guys through that nasty swamp and go around the possible ambush. Besides, wasn't it you, Hollywood, who was hiding in the last fire fight we were in?"

"I wasn't hiding. I got heat prostration and I couldn't move."

"The sun doesn't shine on me or what? You're just a chicken-shit." The GIs laugh at Ese's comments.

The lieutenant approaches the soldiers and asks, "What seems to be the problem here, Sergeant Three Bears? The rest of the battalion is waiting for your platoon to lead us out of here."

"We ain't going sir."

"What? Sergeant Three Bears, you are one of the best soldiers in the battalion. The captain has even talked about giving you a battlefield commission. I hate to see you go to prison for something like this," says the lieutenant.

Before Three Bears can reply, the captain arrives. "What's going on here, lieutenant? Why isn't your platoon moving out?" he asks.

"We ain't going, sir," says Three Bears. Then he explains to him why.

"I said move out," orders the captain. The radioman interjects, "Sir, the battalion commander wants to know what the problem is."

"Tell him there isn't any problem. We're moving out now, right, Sergeant Three Bears?" says the captain as he looks at the men, and notices that he has a serious problem on his hands. He thinks, this dirty redskin and little fucking greaser are going to cost me my promotion.

"No sir," says Three Bears.

As much as he dislikes talking to officers, Ese nevertheless tells him, "Captain, I'll lead the battalion through the swamp or river, anywhere but the same path we've taken the last two days."

"Sir, the Colonel says he is coming to investigate," announces the radioman.

"Men," the captain begins, "we have a job to do and it is our duty to fulfill it. We have all been through some tough times together. Don't believe your country doesn't appreciate all of your sacrifices. But we need resolve if we are going to stop the communists from taking over the world and our country."

Shit, ponders Ese, The Vietnamese don't even have a navy. How can they attack the U.S.?

"I can understand your feelings about an ambush," the captain continues, "I have the same feelings, but the possibility is always there no matter where we're at. Our duty is to engage the enemy and defeat him on the battlefield, because infantry is the queen of battle," finishes the captain as boldly as possible.

"The colonel is here," announces the radioman.

An athletic middle-aged soldier walks up to the captain and demands, "What's the problem here, captain?"

"It's just a small problem, sir, nothing I can't take care of, sir."

"I heard that some of your men don't want to move out."

"That's right, colonel," says Three Bears respectfully. "If you give me one minute, I can explain to you why."

"I've already had it explained to me, sergeant. I don't need any lower echelon personnel telling me what to do," orders the colonel with contempt.

"But, sir, we don't think it's..."

"That's enough, sergeant," snaps the colonel, his face flushed red with contempt, his jugular vein throbbing with blood.

"Fuck it then, you fucking squirrel-headed bastard," blasts Three Bears with ferocity. "We ain't going in, right guys?"

Ese nods his head and so does the rest of the squad.

"You men," the colonel points to Three Bears and his squad, "are going to be court-martialed for disobeying a direct order, and for cowardice in the face of the enemy. Consider yourselves under arrest. All right, lieutenant, move your platoon out," he orders. "We'll take care of these cowards when this operation is over."

Kool Aid, one of the most decorated soldiers in the platoon, is the first to break the ranks of the potential mutineers. Many soldiers are still undecided, but once the first man moves out, the majority feel morally obligated to follow. One by one, the men follow. Three Bears, Marlon, Shorty, Da-Da, Cadillac, Beaucoup and Ese watch their friends pass them by: Snake, Hero, Socks, Bubba, Canteen, Indio, Chulo, Teacher, Poontang, Daffy, Scratch, Pirate, Perf, Chato, Seahorse, Baby, Chon, Rubber-Face, Slick, Sunshine, Hollywood, Sham, Skate, Butter, Crazy, Deadwood, Fingers, Shadow and Mudhen. After them follow the three hundred odd soldiers that they don't know by name. In the middle of the file is the colonel and his staff. No one says anything or looks at Ese's squad as they pass by them.

Ese surmises, these are dead men. They know something is wrong and can feel death.

After all the soldiers pass, Three Bears and his squad are the last to join in. The reason that they join in is because the whole battalion is moving out to a new base camp and they can't stay behind by themselves.

After the battalion has gone out a kilometer, the ambush Beaucoup predicted is set in motion. It is an inverted "L" shaped ambush, composed of North Vietnamese and Viet Cong elements. They are dug in about twenty meters from the thrice used trail, armed with AK-47's, M-1's, M-16's, M-60's, thirty caliber machine guns, mortars, and anything else they can muster. The first fifty U.S. soldiers are killed instantly. The bullets hit the GIs from different angles with such velocity that they are suspended in the air like dangling puppets on erratic strings.

The battalion commander manages to call in artillery. The enemy is dug in so close to the GIs that most of the artillery falls on them. 155 millimeter rounds, packed with forty pounds of explosives, begin to blow the soldiers apart. Heads, arms, legs, and torsos fly like loose ground meat in a hurricane.

Ese is walking behind Beaucoup when the ambush begins. A bullet hits Beaucoup in the midsection and he falls like a deflated rubber doll. Three Bears is walking behind Ese when he is struck by shrapnel in his thigh and a bullet in his pelvis. He is knocked unconscious by sheer pain. Shorty is shot in the head and dies instantly.

Ese, Da-Da, Cadillac and Marlon are the only ones in the file that are not hurt. Ese asks them to help him move Beaucoup and Three Bears from the scene. Three Bears' pants are imbued with blood. He begins to regain consciousness as Ese drags him from behind, with his arms under Three Bears' armpits and hands locked across his chest.

"We got to get out of here, buddy. Just hang on. Help's on its way. Just think of all the pussy you're going to get back in the world. You'll be laying in the cut bigger than shit. Yeah, you are. Just hang on. We've even got some morphine for you. We'll give it to as soon as we can find a hideout. You're going to feel so good you won't even need a chopper to fly away. You'll be riding the Gravy Train with biscuit wheels," says Ese as he drags Three Bears.

Three Bears eyes are rolled back as Ese's voice seems to be coming from a cloud.

Cadillac lifts Beaucoup and carries him away in a firemans' carry. Da-Da covers them as they retreat. Ese scans the terrain as he drags Three Bears. The closest place for a hiding place is a few meters away, in the swamp the colonel didn't want to cross. They conceal themselves in a muddy swamp surrounded by brier.

"O.K., fellas, it's party time," says Cadillac as he prepares to inject Beaucoup and Three Bears, who have both regained consciousness, with morphine. A sigh of relief is given by both soldiers as the narcotic takes effect. Cadillac takes Ese by the side and whispers, "Beaucoup is losing a lot of blood. If we don't get him to a hospital soon, he's a goner. And maybe Three Bears, too."

"I know," answers Ese. "We've got to get a radio so we can call for a helicopter. The radioman was about five guys ahead of Beaucoup. Me and Da-Da will go back and see if we can retrieve the radio. Let's go, Da-Da," orders Ese, who is now in charge because he has the most rank.

Without the wounded, they retrace their path much quicker than before. At the ambush site, the file of dead and wounded soldiers is more than a kilometer long. The Vietnamese have not yet reached the end of the file.

From a short distance, they see North Vietnamese soldiers dressed in standard issue, green uniforms. The Viet Cong are dressed in black pants and shirts with black and white checkered scarfs around their necks.

Ese low-crawls up to the dead radioman and recovers the radio. He falls back to where Da-Da is at. When the Vietnamese reach the end of the file, Ese and Da-Da see them check everybody to see if they are alive. The enemy shoots the wounded in the head or stabs them with bayonets—stainless steel bayonets with triangle sides of curled, protruding barbs, outlawed by the Geneva Convention. They watch as the VC stab the wounded and pull out their intestines by the barbs. Marlon is one the soldiers that is still alive and bayoneted.

"Pobre Marlon, he never wanted to kill anyone," murmurs Ese.

In disbelief, they see the enemy cut open some of the GIs, yank out their livers and take a bite of them. Ese watches with his mouth open and shudders as he contemplates, What am I doing here? "Why'd they do that, Da-Da?" he asks.

"From what I heard these guys believe that if they eat the livers of their enemies, their enemies' warrior spirit will transfer to them," whispers Da-Da.

"Let's get the flock out of here," says Ese.

When they return to their hideout, Cadillac tells them, "Beaucoup is dead."

"He was a good guy," says Ese as he stares at Beaucoup's body stretched out lifeless, with invading flies using his mouth as an air terminal. "If that stupid colonel would've listened to us, none of this would have happened. We would've fucked them guys up. That bastard and Hollywood deserved to die, but not the other men. If the colonel weren't dead, I'd probably kill him myself."

"I got Di An, Essay," says Cadillac. "They want to know our coordinates. I don't think they believe what happened to us."

"Give me the horn," says Ese. "Look, asshole, we need help, everybody got wiped out."

"Don't you know anything about radio discipline, soldiers?" asks an officer angrily. "Just hold on and keep your heads down. We're going to artillery the area to chase the enemy away. Then we're going to send reinforcements."

"Chase away? Why, those dudes have done gone under their tunnels." When Cadillac finishes speaking, artillery falls on the ambush site.

"The only thing that artillery is doing now is blowing our guys up more," says Da-Da.

After the artillery barrage, Three Bears begins to stir. "Where am I?"

"You're dead and you're in the happy hunting grounds," replies Ese.

"Now that I see your mug, I know I'm in hell," says Three Bears smiling. "I can't move."

"Relax. Reinforcements are coming," says Ese. He pulls out a small plastic bag and pulls out a marijuana cigarette. He lights it and places it on Three Bears' lips.

Three Bears inhales and says, "Oh, that feels good."

Ese reaches in the bag again, takes out a small hair and places it in Three Bears mouth. "Swallow this, it'll give you strength."

Three Bears swallows the hair. After Ese gives him water to drink, he says, "Thank your girlfriend for me. You've got a woman that loves you. Don't lose her asshole."

"Here come the helicopters," says Da-Da. As the infantry lands, Cadillac is in constant communication with them. When Cadillac is convinced that they can safely leave their hiding place without being shot by their own men, they come out carrying Three Bears in a poncho-made stretcher."

"Shit, you've got to lose weight, Oso. Now I know you were the one who was stealing my candies from my pack. Huh, asshole?" says Ese.

"Boy! Are we glad you guys came to our rescue!" says Cadillac when he meets the rescuers. "We need a medevac."

"One is on the way," says a captain.

Ese's constant attention is on Three Bears. "Except for your ugliness, I wish I were you, Oso. In no time at all, you're going to be back in the world, getting all them fine women and drinking wine. You'll be sleeping in a clean bed and getting three squares a day. Listen, here comes the helicopter for you."

The medevac helicopter lands. Ese helps rush Three Bears to the helicopter. They hastily throw Three Bears on the helicopter. Holding back their manly emotions, Ese and Three Bears look at one another for the last time.

Ese stays in place staring at the helicopter flying away. "Let's move out sergeant," orders the captain. "Show us where the rest of your battalion is."

"Yes sir. But can I go and retrieve our dead Vietnamese advisor?," asks Ese.

"We don't have any time to go and pick up any dead gooks, sergeant. Move out."

"Pinche puto," says Ese.

"What did you say?" asks the captain.

"I said, 'it is good to be alive,' in Spanish, sir."

When they reach the first casualties, the survivors recognize some of the dead. Many are blown apart by enemy bullets and U.S. Army artillery. Other bodies are intact with bullet holes in their temples or their intestines and stomachs ripped out.

When Ese, Da-Da, and Cadillac go down the line, the spirits of the dead emanate an effusion of tender comfort and understanding. They feel an affinity with the dead. This sensitivity makes it much easier for them to pick up the pieces of their comrades.

It is difficult at times to identify which parts belong to what person. For the lack of a better system, equal amounts of body parts are placed in each body bag. Towels or bits of blown uniforms are used in place of gloves to pick up bloody pieces of flesh. Most of these bodies will later be placed in sealed caskets. Their families and friends will never know that it is a collage of soldier remains in the coffins.

At the funeral ceremonies grieving families will be consoled by a picture, sitting on top of the coffin, of the soldier in his Class-A uniform taken during basic training. These families will be forever haunted by doubts of whose remains were in the coffin. Many of the spirits will return to their homes and appear to their people in dreams and mild hallucinations to inform them that they are indeed dead. Nevertheless, more than one mother will inevitably die from grief.

Ese, Da-Da and Cadillac are now part of the company that has come to their aid. Given what they have gone through, the company commander allows them to have the first guard. All three soldiers are in sedated shock and cannot sleep.

All night long, Ese reflects, What am I doing here? These guys ain't ever going to invade the United States. I don't even know these Vietnamese vatos. I kind of even look like them. They're mostly farmworkers just like my family. What am I doing in this gringo army? This is the same army that took the land away from our people. When I get home, I'll just be another greaser. Fuck this war, fuck the gringos and the horses they rode in on, too.

What should I do now? Refuse to fight? Naw, I've only got three months left to go in country. And anyways, prison ain't no place to be. Maybe I should join the Viet Cong? How could I join them? They'd kill me. And even if I could join them, I would never be able to go home again. Naw, that ain't going to get it. Besides, I'm on this side right now and I can't be a traitor. I guess the best thing to do is not walk point anymore, and just try to survive these last three months. I won't take no more extra chances, he decides.

The next morning, after the rest of the bodies are policed, Ese has a chance to write the familiar letter to his mother.

Hi Mom:

I got your package the other day y estaba muy suave.[5] Everything is coming along O.K. Just the same type of weather, real hot. Right now we are at the beach y está muy bonito.[6] I also got a package of chili beans and tortillas from tía Mona. Es todo por mientras.[7] I'll see you in three months.

Your Son

---

5. and it was real good.
6. and it's very beautiful.
7. This is all for now.

EPISODE XXVI
There Ain't no Tamales in Viet Nam

Wino is walking the point for the platoon up a well-used, steep trail. Ro-Ro is his backup man. When they reach the top of the mountain, they take a short break next to some large rocks. Smoking cigarettes, Wino and Ro-Ro watch the trail leading down the mountain. At the foot of the mountain is a meandering stream. Chuco comes up and joins Wino and Ro-Ro. "Tienes el bote de pintura?"[1] Ro-Ro asks Chuco.

"Sí, aquí está," says Chuco as he reaches inside his rucksack and pulls out an army issue spray paint can and hands it to Ro-Ro. After shaking the can, he writes graffiti, Chicano style, on the rocks. The first thing he writes is: El Ro-Ro loco de Xicali y que. Then he writes: Que chinguen sus madres los chinos.

"Pasame el bote,"[2] asks Wino. Ro-Ro hands it to him and he writes, El Wino con mi ruca la Trucha PV, followed by: la raza no se raja.[3]

"Como estas loco, Wino. Pasame el bote. It's my turn," says Chuco. Next to El Chuco de Califas, he writes Mao Tse-Tung es joto y Ho Chi Minh es chavala.[4] "This will piss the gooks off," he says. After the break, the word is given to move down the mountain. Wino and Ro-Ro know that ambushes and enemy camps are frequent near streams and rivers, so they move slower than usual.

They reach the bottom of the mountain and cross the stream. Suddenly, the cracking of AK-47s burst out. Wino is killed by a bullet

---

1. "Do you have the can of paint?"
2. Slick Ro-Ro from Mexicali. Then he writes: The Chinese can fuck their mama's
   "Pass me the can,"
3. Wino with my girl Trucha for life, followed by: Mexicans don't back down.
   "Your crazy Wino. Pass me the can.
4. Chuco from California, he writes: Mao Tse Tung is a queer and Ho Chi Minh is a sissy.

to the chest. His only reaction is a painless sigh, "Ah." Ro-Ro is shot in the belly and legs. He manages to drag himself forward, away from the stream. A fierce fire fight ensues. Chuco brings his M-60 machine gun up and begins to lay a solid base of fire.

Across the stream, Ro-Ro gathers himself and takes cover behind a log. In front of him is a tiny meadow. The enemy is well protected by a tree line ahead of them, and they are dug in too close to call in artillery or mortars on them. They sporadically shoot back at one another for a while.

At times, Ro-Ro is able to talk to the platoon. "Sacame de aquí.[5] I'm losing a lot of blood y me duele un chingo." [6]

"We can't get across, compa. Wait till it gets dark y luego te puedemos ayudar.[7] Don't worry, we can keep them from getting to you," shouts Chuco.

The fire fight slackens and the opponents are in a stalemate. Nightfall comes and Ro-Ro surmises as he sees the moon rise, Lo sabía,[8] there's going to be a full moon tonight; that's as bad as daylight. "Chuco, ayudame," [9] he yells.

"Ay te voy, compa," shouts Chuco as he attempts to cross the stream, but is deterred by bullets. "I can't get across compa, but we can see them if they try and get you.'

"¿Que le paso al Wino?" [10] he asks.

"Le dieron en la madre," replies Chuco.

"Ayudame, Chuco me duele un chingo," says Ro-Ro.

---

5. "Get me out of here.
6. "It hurts like hell."
7. Then we can help you.
8. "I knew it,
9. Chuco help me,"
   "Here I come buddy,"
10. "What happened to Wino?"
   "They killed him,"
   "Help me Chuco, it hurst like hell,"

Again Chuco tries to reach Ro-Ro, but is stopped by bullets.

"Ayudame Chuco, me duele un chingo." Ro-Ro says again with pain.

"Órale, no te aguites,[11] just hang on; the choppers are going to come with more vatos to help us. When they get here, te vamos a dar some real good grifa, un buen tequilla y unos tamales de aquellotas." [12]

"Ya ni la chingas, there ain't no tamales in Viet Nam!"

"Yes there are. I didn't show you but my jefita[13] sent me some in a can. I still have them. Y también, aquerdate de las nalgotas de Nena que te esperan en Mexicali." [14]

"¿Órale buey, como sabes que Nena has a big butt?" complains Ro-Ro.

"You've only shown us her picture a million times. No te apures, I won't let the gooks get to you, cuñado," [15] Chuco reassures him as he lets out a burst of machine gun fire. "Vez. Why don't you sing a song, a song that will help."

"Sing a song, are you stupid? Who are you, Mitch Miller?"

"Come on, sing a song. One of your favorite ones."

"Que sera, sera," Ro-Ro begins to sing.

"Parale ay, compa," [16] interjects Chuco. "If you keep singing that shit, we're going to shoot you ourselves," Chuco tells him, as a humorous psychology ploy to lift Ro-Ro's spirits. "Canta algo[17] that reminds you of the good times when you were a happy little chavalio." [18]

"Si. That's right. Me aquerdo[19] when I was a chavalio and the gringa teacher used to give us cookies and milk y cantabamos, 'Jimmy...

---

11. "Don't feel down,"
12. we are going to give you some real good weed, fine tequila and excellent tamales
13. mom
14. And also remember Nena's big butt that waits for you in Mexicali."
  "Hey asshole, how do you know Nena has a big butt,"
15. Don't worry
16. "Stop it buddy,"
17. "Sing something
18. kid
19. I remember

Jimmy ...crack corn... and I don't... care. Jimmy ...crack corn... and I don't care.' Or sometimes...cantabanos, 'Zipp...edy do...da, Zipp...edy ay. My...oh...my, wh...at a won...der...ful day. Zipp...e...dy do...da. Zipp...e...dy ay.' " he sings slowly and sadly.

"Yeah, keep singing like that Ro-Ro. Tú eres chingon." [20]

"Chuco...Chuco, I'm losing a lot of sangre, carnal," [21] he says with agony.

"No te aguites,[22] sing another song."

"La cuca..ra...cha, la cuca...ra...cha, ya no pue...de ca...minar. La cuca...ra...cha, la cuca...ra...cha, ya...no...pue...de ca...min...ar. Por...que...le... fal...ta ..., por...que...le...fal...ta.., mari...jua...na...que fu...mar," [23] finishes Ro-Ro with his eyes staring at eternity.

---

20. Your a bad dude."
21. blood, brother,"
22. Don't feel down,
23. The cockroach can't walk...the cockroach can't walk...because it needs..., because it needs, marijuana to smoke.

EPISODE XXVII
Getting Short

"Three days and a wake up, and I'm home free. I'm getting shorter than your dick, Machete," says Pepsi while wiping the sweat from his forehead with a towel.

"I'll be right behind you following your trail home," answers Machete. "Why don't you ask the captain to let you go back to the rear on today's re-supply chopper?"

"I ain't asking that sorry son-of-a-bitch for nothing. The only guys he does anything for are those suck-asses of his: The ones that carry his water, make his coffee, and kiss his ass. I've come this far without his West Point stupidity. I figure I can make it for a couple of more days."

"The only good captain we had was Jack Flash, but he's dead now. He's the only captain that ever cared about his men. Hellfire, ain't that some shit. I just thought of something; I won't even be able to buy any beer when I get back home. As a matter of fact, I won't even be able to vote for the motherfuckin' politricking, trick-or-treating politicians that came out with those bogus laws in the first place, just cause I ain't twenty one."

Pepsi begins thinking good thoughts about corn. Partly because he's from Nebraska, but mainly because he's hungry, he hankers for corn and everything you can possibly make out of it. He thinks of corn on the cob, cornbread, cornmeal, cornflakes, corndogs, buttered popcorn, even corn-fed hogs.

Throughout the day, Pepsi plans of all the things he's going to do. First of all, he has not told his family or fiancée what day he's coming home, so it will be a complete surprise to them. He'll call his girl when he is leaving the airport from San Francisco to pick him up at the

Omaha Airport. From there, he'll take her to a motel and make love to her. Maybe they can even start trying to have a baby that same day.

When they leave the motel, they will go to his mother's house. He hopes it will be a Sunday when he arrives in Omaha, so everybody will be home. And with luck, it'll be in the evening and his mother will have cooked a nice Sunday dinner as is the custom in their household. He can just taste the baked ham she likes to make.

He can't believe he's going home in two days and leaving the war behind him. It will be the end of his Viet Nam calamity. No more living like an animal. No more killing. He'll get married that summer and start college on the GI bill that fall. He concludes that everything is going to be so good when he gets back to the world.

Pepsi has not walked point for two weeks. He does not want to take any unnecessary chances, so he walks in the middle of the file. The day goes by without incident. Shortly before sundown, the company stops to rest for the night. Pepsi is obsessed with his plans. "Hellfire, I'm fucking tired," he tells Machete, as he takes his rucksack off and goes down to sit on the ground.

A loud explosion sends Pepsi flying up in the air when he sits down. His mangled body falls limp to the ground. Machete is hit with shrapnel. He rolls from side to side on the ground from deep pain. His intestines hanging out of his belly pick up dirt and dry grass. "Me duele, me duele,"[1] he says over and over again. When he is able to stop rolling, he lies dazed on the ground, holding his protruding intestines with his hand and staring at Pepsi's dead body.

---

1. "It hurts, it hurts,"

EPISODE XXVIII
Change of Mind

Ese has decided not to be the pointman anymore. He made up his mind when he last talked to Da-Da and Cadillac two days earlier. He told them, "Man, I sure am glad you guys are going home tomorrow. I wish I was going with you. Why, you could even come to my mom's house and have an enchilada dinner while you waited for your discharge papers. My house is only a two-hour drive from Oakland."

"Don't worry, Essay. In a month, you're going to be on your way back to the world," assures Cadillac. "Just quit walking the point and keep these guys in line 'cause they don't know whether to shit or go blind. Can you believe it? In less than a week, if the good Lord is willing and the creek don't rise, I'll be in Augusta, GA, drinking bourbon and doing the funky chicken," said Cadillac

"You're right, Cadillac. I won't walk point anymore. I don't want to be a hero anymore," said Ese. "Fuck this fucked up army. Fuck the gringos and the horses they rode in on, too."

Nearly all the people that Ese had come to know in Viet Nam are dead or have gone home, many of them badly wounded. A vacuum fills his heart and he feels like crying. No seas culo,[1] he says to himself while holding back tears. An overpowering loneliness takes hold, rendering him emotionally helpless.

"Get ready to move out, sergeant," orders the company commander walking into Ese's bunker. Your platoon is going to go and help Delta company. They were hit hard about an hour ago. Don't tell the new lieutenant this, but I want you to take charge of the platoon. You know he dropped out of the seminary where he was studying to be a

---

1. Don't be an asshole,

185

priest? Good guy, but not one to be trusted with your platoon yet. And those shake-and-bake sergeants straight from the NCO academy are no help."

"Yes sir," says Ese reluctantly. "I think he's right," figures Ese as the captain walks out. "I should also be pointman because, except for sergeant Gumby and Youngster, the radioman, everybody is new. If a new guy takes the point, it's for sure he won't know when he's walking into an ambush. So that only leaves me for point because Gumby and Youngster have to call and direct mortars and artillery, medevacs too, if we need them."

Today is my day to get hit, portends Ese. I know it is. I just hope I don't get killed. And I'm praying they don't shoot, as Gypsy said, "my hamster dick" off. Besides, it would be nice to get a chance to kill a few more motherfuckers before I leave, thinks Ese, putting aside his decision not to fight for the white man anymore, as he prepares his weapon.

When Ese walks outside the bunker, the lieutenant and the shake-and-bake sergeants are waiting for him in full-combat gear. Ese realizes that most of the soldiers are white and they are waiting for him to give the orders. Shit, I sure was stupid to believe all that bullshit about Mexicans being dumb. Look at all these gringo putos waiting for me to tell them what to do, reflects Ese. Ese briefs the lieutenant and sergeants on what to expect and the tactics they will use in going into the ambush area.

After the briefing, Ese's platoon is airlifted to the ambush site by helicopter. Unlike other missions, where Ese hoped that the flight would take longer, he now wishes the helicopter would travel faster. He is anxious to meet his fate and to get the pain over with as soon as possible. I only have one of Chanclas' pelos left. If everything comes down real hard, like I think it will, I'm probably going to need more than one hair to keep me alive. I guess one pelo is better than nothing, he reckons.

Ese is in the lead helicopter and is the first one to get off. He begins to secure a perimeter. "We're only a couple of kilometers away from the ambush site where our battalion got wiped out and my pal, Oso-Bear, got fucked up," he tells the thin sergeant, Gumby, while they wait for the new lieutenant to wander around the perimeter, acting like he knows what he is doing.

"I think we can move out now, sergeants," says the lieutenant.

Ese stares at the crew-cut on the young lieutenant and concludes, Pobre criatura.[2] This poor kid is hurting personnel.

"Sergeant, I think we ought to move out in double files toward our objective like they taught us in Officer Candidate School," he tells Ese.

"No, sir, that's not the way we work around here," says Ese matter of factly while he and Gumby clasp wrists, helping Ese up off the ground. "Just follow me and you'll get out of here alive."

Ese leads the platoon toward the interior of the jungle. Gorgeous, aromatic orchids hang from vines. Tropical plants with huge, green leaves expel fresh oxygen, providing the soldiers a quick rush to their brains. Ese passes the word down the line to be extra careful because he knows that this Shangrila landscape cloaks death. Stealthily, he makes his way into the core of the jungle. Ese has learned to blend in with the jungle; every step and move is in unison with the pulse of the environment. His breathing is in rhythm with the inhalation and exhalation of the vegetation. Every blink of his eyes is in tune with the slightest move in front of him. His M-16 has become a part of his body.

Eventually, he runs into a well-used trail. He gives a hand signal to

2. Poor child.

stop and whispers to Jelly Bean, the man behind him, for the lieutenant to come up. Ese winces when the lieutenant comes up stumbling and making all sorts of racket. He whispers to the lieutenant, "You wait for the platoon here. Jelly Bean and me will go check out the trail. Be sure you have someone watching the other end of the trail." As soon as he finishes his sentence, Ese spots some Viet Cong coming up the trail. He sees them before they see him because he has positioned himself and the lieutenant a couple of feet from the trail and in the shadows of the trees.

Ese can't decide whether to tell the rest of the platoon that the VC are coming up the trail, or if he should fire them up first so he can claim some confirmed kills. He decides to shoot at the VC first and kills the first two men coming toward him. "Got the sons-a-bitches," he says. "Bring the platoon up here so we can lay a good base of fire in case the VC want to try and overrun us," he tells the lieutenant.

The sounds of automatic rifles and machine guns interrupt the feral tranquility of the jungle as humans once again begin to kill and maim themselves. "Pass me the thump gun," Ese yells down the line. "I know where some of them are." An M-79 grenade launcher is passed to him He braces the butt of the stock up to his shoulder and pulls the trigger. At once, he feels a tremendous, sharp pain to his head. Holding his hands around his eyes, he falls down and says, "sons-of-a-bitch," The pain is quickly replaced by a comprehensive infinity. Ese no longer feels his body. In his mind he sees snapshot colors intertwined with black and white, of the many soldiers that he has seen shot above the waist and, except for one, all died.

Ese talks to God and asks to let him live Then, he envisions himself on his knees picking cotton without wages for the rest of his life. Visions of his mother are followed by pain as he comes back to life.

Jelly Bean has been talking to Ese while he is in shock. "Hang on, help is on the way," he tells Ese.

"Oh shit, I can't see," says Ese grabbing his eyes, kicking and squirming with pain.

"You got hit with shrapnel in the head. Some nerves to your eyes must of gotten hit. Medic, Medic!" yells Jelly Bean.

The medic, a boyish-looking soldier, quickly responds. He deftly applies direct pressure to Ese's four wounds. One of the wounds is especially severe. The medic can see parts of Ese's skull. This guy has some mean wounds, he calculates. He cleans and bandages the wounds the best he can.

"Give me some fucking morphine, Doc. The pain is killing me."

"I can't do that. It's against procedure; no morphine for head wounds."

"Fuck procedure. Give me some morphine." Ese's request goes unheeded.

The fire fight intensifies. Ese hears and feels bullets whiz by. I'm fucking blind and I can't defend myself. Man, if these putos overrun us, I can't even fire back. Hijo de la chingada, I'm in a world of fuck, he thinks.

Incredibly, after the fire fight is over, Ese is the only one wounded. Night falls swiftly, making it difficult for a helicopter to pick Ese up. Ese is in extreme pain and he vomits from it. After a while he has nothing left to regurgitate and gets the dry heaves. This exacerbates the agony because, since he is forced to try and heave from his empty stomach, his face muscles tighten up, applying more pressure to the wounds. As the misery worsens, the dry heaves intensify, causing more torment. Jelly Bean tries to keep Ese from making noise by placing a towel over his mouth.

After what seems like a lifetime, the dry heaves cease. Ese whimpers and snivels the rest of the night. Right before dawn, he passes out from misery and exhaustion. He wakes up in worse pain than before. "I need a beer, Oso-Bears," he says deliriously. "It hurts worse than fuck, Oso-Bears. But don't worry, I'll make it out alive," murmurs Ese as he rips the bandages off his face and is astonished that he can see again. "I can fucking see, I can see," he says, with relief.

"The helicopter is on its way. Can you hear it?" Jelly Bean asks Ese. "They're coming closer. Listen."

Ese becomes more conscious and hears the faint sounds of the thumping helicopter blades and says, "I hear them. I'm hurting worse than a motherfucking fuck, but I hear them. How in the hell is that chopper going to land? The jungle is too thick."

"Here comes the chopper now. Let me help you up," says Jelly Bean lifting Ese by his left arm. "We're going to get you out by jungle pene-trator. The chopper is right above us now. Here comes the rope with the vest attached to it. Here, let me help you put it on."

Jelly Bean has changed Ese's bandages three times throughout the night. Contrary to standard operating procedure, Youngster and the new lieutenant donated their first aid bandages to Ese. In doing so, Youngster and the lieutenant are now left without clean bandages for themselves in case they are wounded.

Ese has lost more blood and needs his bandages changed again. He puts his hand to his head before he puts his arms through the vest. Fuck, the bandages feel like they've been dried in grape syrup. And I'm dripping worse than a newborn baby with diarrhea, he thinks. I really need to get the fuck out of here. As he thinks that, Ese suddenly feels himself plucked off the ground by the helicopter. Halfway up, the pulling stops. He feels himself swinging back and forth in the air. After a few moments, he is slowly lifted up again.

When he reaches the side entrance of the helicopter, the medics pull him in. "What happened? Why did you stop pulling me up?" he asks the medics.

"The jungle penetrator broke and we had to pull you up by hand," yells one of the medics as the helicopter flies away.

EPISODE XXIX
Chuco's Fate

Chuco is drinking a beer in the kitchen with Comal. "Así pasó Comal, así murió Ro-Ro,"[1] says Chuco ruefully after he recounted how Ro-Ro died. El era unos de mi mejores amigos.[2] When he died it was the first time I cried over here."

"Que pinche aguite,"[3] says Comal, shaking his head.

"Well, at least he fucked up the captain."

"Si, siquiera,"[4] says Comal, nodding his head in approval. "Ten aquí estan unos tacos."[5]

Chuco takes the food and puts it in his rucksack. "Gracias, Comal. Our squad is going out on a recon mission. I'll see you when I get back. Adios," says Chuco, walking out the door.

"Adios, Chuco, y cuidate."[6]

Chuco has regained his sergeant's rank and is in charge of his squad. He leads his squad out of the base camp in the late afternoon. The humidity has gotten worse and the soldiers sweat accordingly. Like all infantry soldiers, Chuco has lost a considerable amount of weight from the time he arrived in country. He also feels much older than his twenty years.

It dawns on him that this is the same path they took on the first mission he went on. He reflects of how much he has changed since he has been in Viet Nam. This is no time to start thinking of all those chingaderas, he muses. I have to concentrate on what is going on

---

1. "That's the way it happened Comal, that's the way he died,"
2. He was one of my best friends.
3. "What a fucking shame,"
4. "Yeah, at least,"
5. "Here take some tacos."
6. "Goodbye Chuco and take care."

right now.

After Chuco feels that they have gone far enough from the base camp, he decides to put up for the night. He makes sure flares and claymore mines are set out around the perimeter and that the guard positions will be manned throughout the night. He shares his position with Champ, a new medic. After he is sure that all things are set for the night, he brings out the tacos that Comal made for him. He shares them with Champ. Champ is amazed that Chuco has tacos out in the field.

The night passes without incident. Chuco doesn't sleep all night long. He feels something missing and can't figure out what it is. I feel empty, he ruminates as he watches the sun begin to sprinkle the earth with light.

"Let's move," he orders the squad. "We've got a lot of humping to do and we've got to meet up with the company ten klicks from here." No sooner has Chuco given the order, when artillery rounds begin to rain on them. "Spread out, everybody spread out!" he yells.

Chuco lays face down and hopes none of the rounds hit him. The ground is thunderous from the impact of the shells. The entire area is pitted with artillery rounds. Chuco feels one round fall next to him and almost passes out from the concussion. He cleans debris of dirt, rock and wood from his eyes and mouth.

The artillery suddenly stops. "Lets get the hell out of here," he shouts. "Vamonos a la verga." He attempts to get up from the ground, but he cannot move. He turns around and he sees his right leg gone from the knee down. The mangled leg looks like hamburger meat. What should I do? Yell? Scream? It doesn't hurt, he mulls. I feel like a towel that has been popped. He lays back down and contemplates as to what he should do next. He figures they need to get out of the area fast.

Champ and another soldier go over to Chuco's aid. When they turn him over on his back, he catches a glimpse of his blown-off foot still in the boot. He props himself on his elbows and sees that only one of the seven other soldiers is wounded.

"We've got to get you out of here fast," says Champ as he applies a tourniquet around Chuco's leg. "I can't give you any morphine, because all of my equipment is blown up. The helicopters won't land around here porque le tienen escame a la artillery.[7] So we've got to carry you away from here."

The other wounded soldier is ambulatory and only Chuco must be carried. Four soldiers grab each corner of a stretcher made from a poncho and tote. They move as fast as they can over a field of tall grass and Chuco hears the comforting, mellifluous, female voice repeating over and over again as he passes-out, wakes-up, passes-out, "Te quiero...I quiero you...te quiero un chingo...I love you."

Chuco's hands are outside the stretcher and bounce on the dry grass. His right leg begins to bleed again like a bottle dripping red wine. Ayudame, tata Dios.[8] Just this one more time. Next time I'll do it on my own, pero por favor ayudame esta vez más, Señor,[9] he prays.

"Here comes the chopper, Chuco," says Champ with exuberance.

"I can't believe it," says Chuco.

The instant the helicopter lands, Chuco is placed in it. The pain becomes worse. The medic aboard immediately gives Chuco a shot of morphine. The pain begins to ease. At last, he concludes. I'm going home. I made it...la hice. He closes his eyes in relief.

When the helicopter lands, two medics quickly carry Chuco off and onto a gurney, and whisk him away to the hospital. Chuco is semi-conscious and begins to fade away. Just as he is about to pass out, a

---

7. because they are afraid of the artillery.
8. "Help me papa God.
9. just help me this one more time, Sir."

jolting pain prevents him from doing so. Once inside the hospital, his clothes are taken off and he is placed on an X-Ray table. The table feels hard and cold. Not able to withstand the pain any longer, he screams, "Put me out, put me out."

"We will as soon as we can, soldier. Just wait a little more," one of the doctors tells him.

Every second moves so slow that time seems to be going backwards for Chuco. The pain is as severe as all the previous wounds except that this time he has not been knocked unconscious. The doctor tells him, "Soldier, we are going to put you under. Count backwards starting from number ten," he tells him as he places a plastic mask over Chuco's nose and mouth. Chuco feels the mask on his face and begins to count from ten, he doesn't quite get to number nine before the merciful anesthesia takes effect.

Chuco wakes up feeling as if he is in the middle of a fire. He stares at the leg cut off below the knee, the shock of losing it has not set in. It will be years before he psychologically concedes that he has lost his leg. "How long have I been out?" he asks a passing medic.

"Two days."

"Where's Biscuits?"

"Who's that?" asks the medic.

"He's a real nice guy. Sometimes he walks a little like a girl," says Chuco.

"Oh, the queer," says the medic snickering.

"That's him. Where is he? He's a buddy of mine."

"Don't tell anybody, but a few days ago, the colonel, you know the one everybody calls colonel Dumbkoff, was drunk and broke his ankle as he was getting off his jeep. Of course, he awarded himself a silver star medal the very next day. He had his own room and one night a nurse walks in unexpectedly and catches him and your friend, Biscuits doing it."

"Where is Biscuits now? In jail?"

"Hell no. He's been reassigned to a sham job in Hawaii to keep him quiet."

"Oh," says Chuco.

After two weeks of recuperating in Viet Nam, Chuco is sent to Camp Zama, Japan to convalesce. He arrives late at night to Camp Zama, the misery and tragedy of all the wracked bodies around him no longer bother him. Since he is now out of the Republic of Viet Nam, he feels a great relief. That night, he sleeps like a bear in hibernation.

In the morning, he wakes up to an annoying feeling at the bottom of his foot. "Que chingados," he says. He sees Machete rubbing the teeth of his comb across the sole of his foot. Standing next to him is Ese with his head bandaged up. "What the fuck happened to you?" he asks Ese.

"Ain't no big thing, carnal. You should have seen me three weeks ago, but the doctors fixed me up real good. They put a steel plate on my chumpeta,[10] and I'm just like brand new. I'm a lot better off than Machete 'cause they had to put a lot of plastic guts in him. I think they even made him a plastic asshole. It's so bad he even shits plastic now. Huh, Machete?"

All three laugh hysterically out of triumphant jubilation because they made it out of Viet Nam alive, maybe not in one piece, but alive. "We've got to go. Our plane is leaving real soon for the world. We'll see you back in Illusion in a few weeks," says Machete, shaking Chuco's hand. Ese still doesn't like shaking hands and just walks away.

Chuco feels a moroseful abyss imploding in his chest, and almost breaks down as he watches Ese and Machete leave.

---

10. noogen

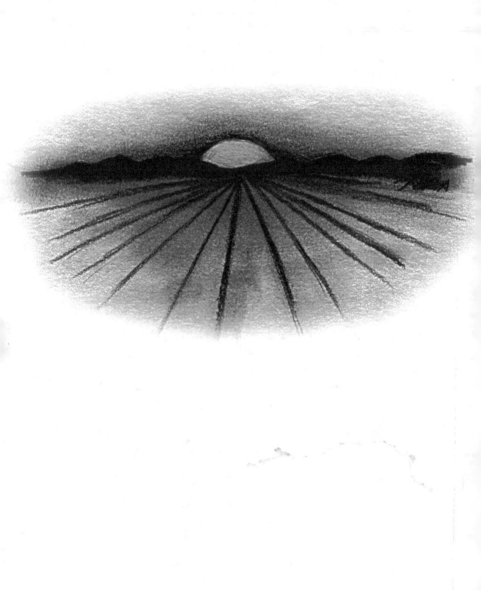

LAST EPISODE
Home to Illusion

Two statuesque figures stand next to a large, overweight contractor at the end of the sugar beet rows, waiting for the last three workers to complete their thinning. Ese, Chuco and Machete are in a race to see who can finish their rows first. "Voy a chingar," yells Machete. This is all the challenge Ese needs to give a last surge to win the contest. When he is out of the row, he stands up facing two Border Patrol agents.

"Where were you born?" asks one agent with disdain.

"Fuck you," he answers, pissed-off.

"What did you say?" asks the other agent, enraged and astonished that a Mexican would talk back to them like that.

"I said, fuck you. Can't you understand Eng—" But before Ese can finish his sentence or set himself to fight back, the agents assault and begin to hit him with macanas.[1]

---

1. billy clubs

Other books offered by Chusma House Publications
ORDER NOW!

ORDER FORM

No. of Copies:

_____ **SOLDADOS: Chicanos in Viet Nam,** narratives by Charley Trujillo $11.95

_____ **CANTOS,** poetry by Alfred Arteaga $7.95

_____ **CARING FOR A HOUSE,** poetry by Victor Martinez $10.00

_____ **UNDOCUMENTED LOVE,** poetry by José Antonio Burciaga $12.00

_____ **IN FORMATION: 20 Years of Joda,** poetry by José Montoya. $17.95

_____ **DOGS FROM ILLUSION** $11.95
        A Viet Nam war novel by Charley Trujillo

_____ **HOW TO MEET THE DEVIL AND OTHER STORIES** $10.95
        Short stories by Ramón Sánchez

Name _____

Street _____

City _____ ZIP _____

(also send $2.45 for 1st copy shipping & handling plus $1.75 for each additional
book-make checks payable to **Chusma House**) allow 2 to 3 weeks for delivery.

Write to:
Chusma House Publications
PO Box 467
San José, CA 95103
(408) 947-0958

CHUSMA HOUSE PUBLICATIONS